THE
LITTLE
BROTHERS
OF
ST. MORTIMER

THE
LITTLE
BROTHERS
OF
ST. MORTIMER

JOHN FERGUS RYAN

A Delta Book
Published by
Dell Publishing
a division of
Bantam Doubleday Dell Publishing Group, Inc.
666 Fifth Avenue
New York, New York 10103

Library of Congress Cataloging in Publication Data

Ryan, John Fergus, 1931–
    The little brothers of St. Mortimer / by John Fergus
Ryan.
        p.   cm.
    ISBN 0-385-30133-2 (pbk.)
    I. Title. II. Title: Little brothers of Saint Mortimer.
PS3568.Y358L5   1991
813′.54—dc20   91-4410
                                                        CIP

Manufactured in the United States of America

Published simultaneously in Canada

October 1991

10 9 8 7 6 5 4 3 2 1

RRC

for
Tom Landis
and
William Gebauer

"If you want to put a dead body where they won't nobody find it, throw it in a hog pen! Hogs'll eat it all, ever bit, bones, teeth, skull, brogans and jumper jacket. They won't be a trace left after a pen full a'hogs goes after it."

—*old Arkansas saying*

ONE

I was born in Romeo, Texas, a little town three miles north of Kissarat and two and a half miles south of Nedsburg. This is known as the Tri-Cities area.

My family was the fourteenth richest in town, as determined by the Busy Fingers Quilt and Garden Club, of which my mother was a member. She never read anything but *Photoplay* magazine and sent me to school every day dressed up in whipcord riding breeches and a necktie, because all her favorite motion picture actors wore them when posing beside their polo ponies.

Nobody in Texas in those days wore a necktie, except the governor, and then only when he was guest of honor at a hanging. I have never witnessed a hanging, but I did see a man put to death in the electric chair at Kent, Texas, when I was fourteen. The sheriff was in charge and he made a little speech to the crowd about how modern times had come to West Texas, and with them, rural electrification, and how that meant it was now possible to use the electric chair on criminals and how that was going to make life better for honest, law-abiding people.

Then he pulled back a curtain and there was a Mexican with a long mustache, strapped into a tall wooden chair, and the sheriff looked at him and said, "I'll bet you're sorry now, Pedro, that you stole that cantaloupe!" and he pulled the switch.

I hated school and I hated my classmates, who did not understand why I dressed the way I did, in clothes that could not be bought anywhere in Bolero County, but which had to be ordered out of the Sears catalog, and who never missed a chance to beat my ass, and I hated the teachers, who were all morons and sorry old church women.

Miss Faucette, my second grade teacher, had been my mother's second grade teacher and my aunt's second grade teacher. She taught it as a fact that Arkansas was the only state mentioned in the Bible and quoted the passage to prove it, ". . . Noah looked out of the *ark and saw* the dove . . ." She taught it as a fact that World War I ended abruptly as the consequence of President Woodrow Wilson's proclaiming a national day of prayer. She was an old fool when she taught me and she must have been nothing but a young fool when she taught my mother, and all the other school teachers in town were on her intellectual level.

School teachers in Texas in those days were paid forty-three dollars a month, with no income during the summer. Miss Faucette worked then as a salesman of magazine subscriptions, and because of her *Reader's Digest* and *Field and Stream* were found in every home in town.

I was reading *Reader's Digest* through, cover to cover, by the time I was ten, reading and understanding, and it was through *Reader's Digest* that I escaped Romeo and got to learn about the rest of the world. The first dirty story I ever read was in *Reader's Digest*. It was called "Sex as a Nazi Weapon" and it was a good one, all about how the Nazis used the women in conquered countries for sexual experimentation, and also to blackmail neutral diplomats.

By the time I graduated from high school, I had read every book in Bolero County, and was known as "the kid with a lot of book learning but no common sense." In another culture, I would have gone on to college and become a lawyer or a college professor, but no one in Romeo ever thought about college, no one even knew how to go about applying to get in one, so I did not ever even give it a try.

Instead, I got a job helping Professor Switzer and his trained bear, Rudy. The Professor and Rudy used to show up every Saturday on the main street corner of Romeo and Rudy would go into his act. The Professor would take the top off a bottle of Orange Crush or 7-Up or Barq's Root Beer, it did not matter which, and hand it to Rudy, who would be standing on his back legs, and wearing a little cap that was held on by a strap under his chin, and Rudy would turn up the bottle and drink it all in one swallow, then throw the bottle aside and the Professor would hand him another bottle and he would drink it all in one swallow. On a typical Saturday afternoon, Rudy would drink ten to fifteen cases of soft drinks.

Rudy always drew a crowd, people who would throw coins at his feet every time he emptied a bottle, people who thought he was the greatest act of all time, people who would rather be there on the curb watching him than to eat when they were hungry. I remember one time, standing next to the mayor of Romeo as he and a crowd were watching Rudy, and I heard him say to someone, "I can't understand why anyone would want to go to New York to see a show when we got all the entertainment right here that's good for us."

My job was to sweep up the broken bottles after each show, and I had to work right there in front of the townspeople, half-wits all, who used to make fun of me while I swept up that broken glass by saying things to me like, "That bear's gonna eat you up, boy," and "You ain't 'fraid of that bear, are you, boy?"

Professor Switzer was a great man. I never exactly understood why he was stuck in Romeo, since he had been born in Europe and spoke three languages and had once trained bears for some circus in France or Spain.

"Rudy is not entertainment," he used to say to me. "Entertainment is opera, a fat woman wearing a hat with bull horns on it, it's Madame Gazzatti-Gazzatti-Gazzatti singing "Vissi d'arte"; entertainment is Toscanini, it's Caruso, it's Weber and Fields!"

He said things like that to me, but he did not say them to anyone else because he could have got in a lot of trouble, saying good things about opera and Weber and Fields in Romeo, Texas.

"These rubes, these dumb animals who stand around and watch Rudy with moronic grins on their faces, their eyes glazed with stupidity, they disgust me!" he said. "This is a dumb town, maybe even worse than Albania."

The Professor was right, Romeo was a dumb town. The mayor of Romeo was once in New York on business. He took the Greyhound bus up there and got in the papers because he got off the bus and looked at his watch and realized he had about two hours before his appointment at some place where he had to sign sewer bonds, and he decided to "walk out to the edge of town and back," for the exercise. He got lost and had to ask a policeman where he was. The papers up there, always looking out for a human interest story, wrote it up big and, as a result, he got invited to a radio quiz program, where he was asked a musical question. The studio orchestra played the first few bars of Beethoven's Fifth Symphony and the quiz master asked the mayor, "Can you tell me the name of that?" "Of course," said the mayor. "That was Classical Music."

Professor Switzer was my first contact with an educated, civilized, and well-traveled man and he gave me my first blow job, when I was about fourteen, and it was great, because he took out his false teeth and really went after it. If there is one piece of advice I would give young men, it would be, try and get a blow job from an old man who can take out his false teeth. I suppose an old woman who could take her teeth out would be just about the same thing, maybe just as good.

When Professor Switzer retired, he sold Rudy to Betty Ned Burns, who was the richest woman in Romeo and who had the only refrigerator in town that worked well enough to keep ice cream. Betty Ned and her sister Beauty Ned were the only children of old man Bernie Ned Burns, who made a lot of money in the twenties sweating Mexicans in his cotton fields. He was also a bootlegger during Prohibition and was the nearest thing Romeo had to a crime lord. Bernie Ned died about the same time Beauty Ned did, both from cirrhosis of the liver, both from sitting on the front porch of their house drinking Salty Dogs, a mixture of gin, 7-Up, and lemon served in a glass with salt stuck to the rim, from daylight to dark. Betty Ned got everything, the house, the cotton fields, the ice house, the Chevrolet dealership, and the picture show. Betty Ned brought Rudy into her house and kept him in a room with a bearproof carpet and had cold drinks delivered in wholesale quantities to the back door. Thereafter, Rudy performed only for society folks, in what was later acknowledged to be the first home entertainment center in town. I tried to get Betty Ned to hire me to clean up the glass but she had a man around the farm already on her payroll and did not give me the job.

I was too young to be drafted in World War II, but by the time of the Korean War, I was just the right age. When the state draft board sent down Romeo's quota, I was not worried because the Mexicans always got drafted first and there was practically no such thing as a white American boy ever drafted out of Bolero County, even at the height of things, even during the Battle of the Bulge. When it got down to it, however, all but two of the Mexican boys failed their physicals, either from being down with TB or having too much brain damage from breathing insect poison in those cotton fields where they all worked. There was nothing else for the draft board to do but take me and two other American boys, Murl Nutt and Foy Tubbs.

Me and Murl and Foy were sent off together to Basic Training at Camp Breckenridge, Kentucky, where we were thrown in with a lot of Italians from Brooklyn, New York, most of them named Nunzio or Gabe. I was surprised at how easy Basic Training was for me, even the running and climbing up ropes, because I had never done anything like it in Romeo, but once I had about three weeks to get in shape, I was running and marching fifteen miles with full pack, along with the best of them.

Foy Tubbs could not handle it. The change was too much for him, he could not adjust to going to the bathroom every morning in front of others and became constipated and it got worse and he took to his bunk on the weekends and finally they had to send him to the hospital to be operated on to remove impacted feces. He was discharged after that and went back to Romeo then later moved to Roy, Texas, where he is now the postmaster.

Murl Nutt took to the army like he was born for it. The physical part of it was nothing to him, since he had never been anything but a gully runner anyway, ranging all over West Texas, with his dogs and rifles, hunting coyote and rabbits. The food was better than anything he had ever had at home, and the chance to get out from under the thumb of his father, old man Pearl Nutt, was the best thing that ever happened to him.

Murl stayed drunk on the weekends and one time, one of those Nunzios pissed into an empty wine bottle until it was filled up, let it cool off to room temperature, then offered it to Murl one Saturday night, when he was sitting on his bunk, talking big about how much better Texas was than New York, and telling all those Italian boys about how much pussy he got back in Romeo, while they were getting none in New York. Murl turned up the bottle of piss and drank half of it without stopping and without noticing it was not wine. After that, those Nunzios ragged him about it all the time and Murl never did much talking about Texas after that.

I have told this story to other men who have been in the army and they have all said the same thing happened to people they knew, so I guess it is just what goes on in the army, like flushing blankets down the commode.

Murl and me got sent to Korea together, where we were assigned to the 20th Infantry Division. Murl was put in a rifle company and was sent up to the Main Line of Resistance, or the MLR, as they called it, where he swapped lead with the

Communists every day. He found it exciting and did not shrink from combat and would probably have ended up with the Medal of Honor, if he had not stepped on a land mine and been blown to bits.

I was assigned to the division air section, where I started out as a clerk, keeping records of the flight hours logged by artillery observers. There were about thirty of them in the section, all second lieutenants, and another thirty, captains and majors, who were the aircraft pilots.

The commanding officer of the section was a lieutenant colonel, who was required by army regulations to submit an evaluation of each officer under his command to headquarters every six months. He was bored by his assignment and used to take one of the observation planes and fly sixty miles south to Seoul every evening to spend the night at the officers club there. The paperwork connected with writing evaluations of sixty officers was a burden that interfered with the colonel's recreation, and after I had been working under his observation about two months, he handed me the forms for evaluating one of the pilots and said for me to put down a few things about the officer that would guide him in writing his evaluation.

The colonel liked what I did, and it was not long before he left all the evaluations to me, who was, at the time, a private. I put myself in the position of my favorite World War II commanding officer, Field Marshal Erwin Rommel, and asked myself every time I sat down to evaluate an officer, what would Marshal Rommel have thought of this man.

I showed no mercy to the drunks, those who were stupid or those who were crazy, and I was hard on any man with a neat mustache or whom I suspected of being religious but I never blew the whistle on a cocksucker. The colonel usually agreed with my evaluations of the officers and signed the forms and sent them off to army headquarters, where they were taken into account when it came time for promotions. I have sometimes wondered what the higher ups would have done if they knew a private was evaluating sixty officers on their fitness for command, but it never got out, it remained our secret. I never

7

thought there was anything wrong with it because the colonel had confidence in me and I have always just considered it sort of a battlefield commission, from private to major in one afternoon.

My other duties made it possible for me to send in requests for my own promotion whenever there was an opening, with the result that I went from private to master sergeant in ten months. When the news of my promotion to master sergeant appeared in the *Friday Siftings,* a weekly newspaper published in Sweet, Texas, I am told people in Romeo read it in disbelief, asking, "Ain't he the boy as used to sweep up after Rudy?"

While in Korea, I got to know a corporal from New York City named Julian Lamont, who had been a hypnotist and a magician in civilian life and he taught me how to hypnotize people and get them to do things that would make other people laugh. I got to be very good at it, even learning to hypnotize Koreans who could not speak English. There was one Korean man I hypnotized whom I could not bring out of it, no matter what I tried, and he was still walking the streets of Pusan, believing he was a chicken who cackled every afternoon at four o'clock, long after I had left the land for good.

I did not appreciate it at the time, but being drafted into the army was a great benefit to me. It got me away from Romeo, Texas, took me to faraway places and gave me self-confidence.

At my request, I was discharged from the army in Tokyo. I should have stayed in the army, since I was a master sergeant, and by now I would be retired on a pension and living in Hawaii or I should have gone back to Texas and entered college on the G. I. Bill, and by now, I would be a rich lawyer, probably a state senator with a bridge or two named after me. But I was ruined for anything stable and steady, and I fear I was born to be a confidence man, or at least, the closest thing to it. For I had not been in Tokyo a week when I signed on as ship's doctor aboard the S.S. *Ramon Suizue,* out of Manila, that carried six passengers on the Rangoon to Pernambuco run, and it was easy, since while a clerk in headquarters I had made copies of the medical credentials of all the doctors in the Mobile Army Surgical Hospital in our division and I had them with me. I selected one from my collection and presented it to the captain, a diploma proving I was Willard Steinkamp, M.D., graduate of the University of Tennessee College of Medicine at Memphis.

I was the only one on board the S.S. *Ramon Suizue* who spoke English. The captain was an ex-Nazi who had been a German tennis star before the war and claimed to be a three-time winner of the Hitler Cup, and the crew, about twenty men, were mostly Filipinos, with a Chinaman or two, and two from South America, either Brazilians or Argentinians.

The job was easy. I had almost nothing to do and I had had enough experience in the army, living in a squad tent with the unit medics, to be able to fake being a doctor, especially among the six passengers, who included a very fat Italian woman who spoke no English and whom I gathered was some kind of countess.

There were no medical problems for the first three days out, beyond treating several of the crew members for venereal diseases, which meant giving them shots of penicillin. After a week out, the Italian countess came down with an infestation of boils on her left hip and came to the sick bay daily for treatment. I knew enough about boils to treat her with antibiotics and antiseptics scrubs and fresh bandages. As the days went on, the boils worsened and required lancing, a job I did to perfection until two days out of Pernambuco, when the ship took a roll as I was plunging the lancet into an angry swelling, and I missed the boil and cut a tendon in her leg.

She ended up a permanent cripple and sued the line that operated the ship but she never blamed me for anything and sent me Christmas cards for several years thereafter, which gave me even more self-confidence and strengthened my feeling that I need never worry about the future, for it was obvious that not only was I smart, and able to adapt to circumstances, but I was also likable.

I was twenty-three years old then. I am now fifty-seven and I cannot exactly tell you where the years have gone or what I have to show for them. I spent several years in New Orleans;

less time in Memphis; Houston; Muskogee, Oklahoma; Waco, Texas; Little Rock, Arkansas; and Panama City, Florida. I was forty-eight years old before I ever got to New York City. I have worked as a mind reader, a carnival hypnotist, a bill collector, a private detective, dean of a Bible college, an aluminum siding salesman, a used car salesman, a house painter, a candy-stand operator. I have sold hot dogs at the baseball games, and for a time, I worked in a meat packing house, stirring up chopped pork guts and spices and gelatin in a big, stainless steel tub until it became something called souse, which some people eat between bread, but which I have never tried and never will as long as I can find anything else to eat. I forgot to mention that I have also been a revival preacher, a veterinarian's assistant, and a fry cook with the Wonder Grill chain.

For the past six years, I have been a merchant, in business for myself. I own a Chevrolet Step Van, five years old, but which runs well, and I live in it and sell out of it. My main line of goods is men's socks, factory thirds and fourths, which I buy by the two-hundred-pound bale from a hosiery mill in South Carolina, and have shipped to a warehouse I own in Benton, Arkansas, where a feeble-minded boy, aged seventeen, puts them up into bundles of six pair, which I sell for a dollar a bundle. The boy is a true half-wit and never gets the right number in a bundle but I keep him on because the state of Arkansas pays me three hundred dollars a month to train him as a "hosiery technician" and because he has a schlong the size of a rag bologna and no family to keep me from going down on it.

I travel the back roads, to the little towns off the interstate highway, try to find a vacant lot or a paved parking area and I stop there and set up shop. When I first started, I was harassed by the local police and the county sheriff in every town, who would force me to buy a peddler's license, which was usually high enough to eat up any profit I might have made.

I put up with the police a few months, then I invented the Little Brothers of St. Mortimer. I knew enough about the mentality of the law in those little towns in the south to know they would not bother me if they thought I had something to do with religion. I hired a sign painter to make the sides of my van to read:

LITTLE BROTHERS OF ST. MORTIMER
TRAVELING MINISTRY

Men's Socks $1.00 a bundle!
Fishing Tackle Repaired
Antique Jewelry Appraised
Indian Relics Bought
and
Sold

POETRY CONTEST!

Child Evangelism

"Your purchase supports our Blind Christian
Children's Home"

It is true, I do sell socks and I do repair fishing tackle and I do buy and sell Indian relics and I do appraise antique jewelry, and usually end up doing some old lady out of her rings and chains by telling her it is gold wash and worth no more than sixteen dollars, maybe twenty. The poetry contest is just a scam I made up to collect contest entry fees from crossroads poets.

I pose as a Child Evangelist to fit in with the culture of the towns I work, to reassure the people there, to maybe even make them think of me as a local boy, since every town I visit has at least one such worthy in residence. I do not know what a Child Evangelist is supposed to do but I am sure you would not have to tail one for more than a day before you found him at a playground, sniffing bicycle seats.

The Little Brothers of St. Mortimer sounds like an order of Catholic Brothers and I do nothing to discourage that notion. I even wear a piece of rope around my waist with a few knots in it to look like part of a monk's wardrobe. As far as I know there never really was a St. Mortimer, but there may have been. The Mortimer I had in mind when inventing the whole charade was Mortimer Snerd, the hayseed dummy of ventriloquist Edgar Bergen. I went from there and developed the outlines of a small brotherhood, all men, all with just one name drawn from the Edgar Bergen and Charlie McCarthy Show on the radio in the thirties and forties.

I am the only one who knows the inside story of the Little Brothers of St. Mortimer and I am the only member. If there were others, their names would be Brother Charles, after Charlie McCarthy; Brother Chase, after the Chase and Sanborn Coffee Company, which sponsored the program; Brother William, after W. C. Fields, who was a frequent guest; Brother Noble, after Ray Noble, an Englishman, who was the bandleader.

For myself, I have chosen the name of the genius who made that whole world possible. I am Brother Edgar.

I weigh three hundred pounds, and am thought of as fat, but I am in good health and can still get it up, although now it is just a Utility and no longer a Roaring or a Blue Steel. I do not like women unless they are young, around sixteen. You usually have to pay those that young, unless you are lucky enough to find one who is truly wild. Last spring, in Joplin, Missouri, I met a girl about twelve who gave me a blow job in exchange for a bundle of socks. She was from a poor family, her father was a retired gutter installer, and she had rotted teeth, nothing but spindles and she nearly tore the end off my pecker before she finished. It was cut up badly and I had to go to the Emergency Room to have them take stitches. The doctor, he laughed, he said most men my age who come in with pecker trouble have a pencil stuck up it to get it hard and they claim they do not know how it got there. Once, even a welding rod. The funniest case he ever had, he said, was a man of seventy who came to the Emergency Room with a ten-inch cucumber stuck up his ass. It was so far in, he said, it had to be snaked out with tongs. And all this in Joplin, Missouri, a small town. I wonder what it is like in the Emergency Room of a town the size of Memphis.

I have not told you everything about me and women, but I will. I like to be spanked by a woman, whipped, maybe, is more like it. Most of the time, it is the only way I can get off. You almost always have to pay for this, since half-wits will not understand it and young girls do not have the arm for it. You need to hire an older woman who is experienced in such, preferably an out and out hooker. I used to know one in Nashville who would whip my ass with a piece of lamp wire if I had the money to pay her. She worked as an exotic dancer at the Belle Meade Adult Theatre. She stayed in a little room and danced around naked and guys on the outside could see her if they put a quarter in a slot. She had to pay the theatre one hundred dollars a day to let her work there. Her money came from tips the guys would give her, usually twenty dollars each, to give them a blow job through a hole in the wall of the booth. She told me she once gave thirty blow jobs in one shift which brought her a profit of five hundred dollars that day, after paying the privilege fee to the theatre. She understood about me and whippings, and always cooperated if I had the money, usually thirty dollars. She is gone now, dead from dope. That girl made five hundred dollars a day, about what a dentist makes a day his first year or so in practice, five hundred dollars a day giving blow jobs and yet never had any money, no house, no clothes, no car, not even a set of plastic dishes, because she was on dope and had a thousand-dollar-a-day habit.

I once met a hooker, and not a bad looking one, even though she must have been nearly thirty, in a small town in Arkansas, Crawfordsville, I think it was, near Memphis, and she asked, did I want to party. By this time, we were in the back of some farm supply store she had the key to and I told her I wanted her to whip my ass with an old, three-foot-long piece of a fan belt I carried around with me. She laughed at me and said, "If I was to cut you just once across your bare ass with that belt, you'd have heart failure, with the color you got in your face, and then there you'd be, dead with your britches down in the back of Cameron's Feed Store and how would I explain that to the High Sheriff?" She was a selfish woman.

I have an assistant who travels with me, some kind of Mexican, named Morales Pittman. At least that is what he is calling himself now, although a man came up to us in Denison, Texas, one time and said he was an old friend of his and called him Juan Wolfe. He is a good driver, he has no bad habits, he does not drink or smoke or take dope and he is as neat as a pin. Sometimes, he will be a plant in the crowd when I am selling socks, he will be what the carnival folks call a shill. He will come up to the van, act like he does not know me, and buy three or four bundles of socks and that will usually get the crowd started.

Morales was doing a twenty-year sentence in the Louisiana State Penitentiary, for killing his girlfriend's lover, right there where he caught him in bed with her, shooting him in the neck, a typical Mexican reaction. The Louisiana State Penitentiary at Angola is the nearest thing to Devil's Island we have ever had in this country. He tells me sometimes about how horrible it was, with at least one man dying there every day, either from being killed by the guards or by the other convicts. Morales says it was common there for people who ran the prison, people like counselors and administrators, to be allowed to check out a prisoner and take him somewhere for the weekend, claiming it was part of a plan to rehabilitate them. He says the assistant chaplain used to check him out on the weekend and take him home and let him screw his wife while he watched, but that other than things like that, being in Angola was the same as being in hell. You have got to admire Morales, being through something like Angola and not coming out crazy or dangerous to others. I got him out; without me, he'd still be there. He came up for parole and I had heard about his case from his mother, from whom I had bought some old gold rings. She showed me his picture, taken when he was about twenty and I decided to try and help him out, in the name of the Little Brothers of St. Mortimer, so I wrote to the parole board and told them I would hire him as a driver and "hosiery technician" if he got out on parole. One thing and another happened and he got out, on condition he work for me and stay out of trouble. I had never met him and had decided I would just let him go his way if he was crazy or would not fit in, but as it turned out, Morales is an easygoing young man, glad to be out of Angola, and grateful to me for making it possible.

He has never stolen a dime from me and has even done me a lot of favors, the biggest one, I guess, being the time he saved me from being cut up by a crazy drunk roughneck in the oil fields outside of El Dorado, Arkansas, who had got it into his head I had swindled his old daddy out of a gold watch. He came at me with a Bowie knife and I would have been done for if Morales had not kicked him in the balls, taken the knife away from him and, cut his ass up with it. We dumped him behind the Sun-Up Lounge on Highway 30, about three o'clock one Saturday morning, and I have never heard another word about it.

Morales said taking knives away from men bigger than you is something you had to learn to do to stay alive in Angola. He must have had a lot of scraps in prison because he has scars all over his body, the biggest one being a grid on his right upper chest, where somebody cut him two times down and then two times across. He speaks English and Spanish, and some German, the Spanish not too good, and whenever he gets excited, he goes into some language that is not true Spanish or true Italian or German but sort of a mixture, with some Latin thrown in.

Morales Pittman was once a Communist. He talks about the time he was living in Hoboken, New Jersey, and could not find a job and wanted to change things, so he went into New York and looked up the Communist Party and told them he wanted to join. A young woman wearing a black beret told him he would have to answer some questions first and she asked him, "If you had two Cadillacs, would you give one to your fellow workers?" Morales said "yes." "If you had two town houses, would you give one to your fellow workers?" "Yes," said Morales. The questions went on down the line like that from yachts, to gold

1 5

watches, to top hats and Morales said "yes" to every one. Then she got down to "If you had two shirts, would you give one to your fellow workers?" "No," said Morales. The woman was shocked. "Why?" she asked. "Because," said Morales, "I *have* two shirts!"

I am thankful I swindled that old woman out of her gold rings, because by doing it I met Morales and he has made things a lot easier for me. Sometimes, he will do all the driving for weeks at a time, allowing me to doze in my bunk in the back of the van, or to sit in the seat next to him and look out at the country roll by. He is a hard worker and still young and good looking enough to pull us out of tight spots when I am totally broke, by working as a hustler, getting palsied old men to pay him twenty to thirty dollars to go down on him.

The only reservation I have about him is his claim he is a pure blood Mexican. They say that no real Mexican man will take it up the ass, something to do with their concept of *machismo,* and for this reason, I believe Morales Pittman is some sort of Duke's Mixture, but it is of no importance to me. "I love anal sex, Gimme a Coon or a Kike or a Greasy Mex," as the old song goes.

TWO

This is the first long narrative I have ever written although I did once write a research paper and actually see it published. I will not go into all that right now since it was a big disappointment, although I probably will later, for I was done a great injustice in connection with it and will never forget it as long as I live.

In this account, I will set down everything that happened to me and Morales Pittman, beginning that day in Como, Arkansas, the fifteenth of August, it was, and in the weeks thereafter, in case anything ever comes up, in case I ever need to explain why I did what I did, in case any of the bodies are ever found, so to speak.

Morales and me had spent the night in a motel in Branson, Missouri, actually registering and paying for the room, which is what we do if I have had a good day selling socks. On days when I do not take in much, we sleep in the van, if it is not too cold, then take showers the next morning in some big motel in the neighborhood. We pull up in the parking lot as early as we can get there and just wait until we see someone leaving his room, putting his bags in the trunk of his car, and then driving off. Most of the time, a man checking out of a motel room will leave the door to the room unlocked, usually even standing open. When we see a room with an open door, we go in and clean up, shave and take a shower, just like we were registered there. Sometimes, we even get to take a little nap in the beds, knowing it will be at least two or three hours before the housekeeper arrives to freshen the room.

We left Branson early and drove south to Como, Arkansas, which was my next scheduled stop. I travel the same route, year after year, staying mostly in Arkansas, but sometimes swinging into southern Missouri, west Tennessee, north Mississippi and, now and then, into east Texas and northern Louisiana. I usually get back to each town about once every year, long enough for the socks I sell to have worn out and need replacement. I have been doing this long enough to have developed contacts in just about every town and I know where to park my van to the best advantage, who I have to oil to do it, where to eat, and where to find the action.

We arrived in Como on that cool, sweet August morning, with the grass still a little wet from the dew and I headed straight for the town square to set up my table and set out the jug.

Como has a population of about fifteen hundred. The town stays in my mind when I am away because of Plumrod's Cafe, home of Filet of Sea Trout à la Gookin and of lemon pie served in wedges big enough to cover a dinner plate, with meringue on top that is never less than seven inches high. If you accidentally get a piece of pie with meringue less than seven inches high, Slovis Plumrod, the owner, will give it to you free.

As we drove along Main Street, I kept my eyes peeled for Plumrod's sign, afraid, as I was every time I hit town, that it might be closed, gone into history, Slovis Plumrod having died of clogged arteries from a lifetime spent eating his own food, or shot dead by his wife when she caught him humping one of the cooks or waitresses.

When I saw the sign, my heart leapt up, as the poets say. It was still open and I told Morales we would sure have supper there tonight.

We were still headed for the square and along the way, we passed the usual small town enterprises, a Texaco station with a sign out front that read "*Two* mechanics on duty"; a grocery store with a sale on "Boil" peanuts in the shell, in hundred-pound bags; a video rental store with a banner claiming to have the latest in "Contemporary Christian Horror Films"; Maola Scoots Salon de Beauty; Spurl Noblin, Jr., State Farm Auto Insurance; a Sears catalog store; a real estate office advertising lots for sale in Snarlhaven Cove; and Kyle Cole Used Auto Sales.

It was Saturday, the day the workers at Allied Pill and Meal Company get paid. Allied Pill and Meal is the only industry in town and its plant looks like four tall silos put up side by side. "Pill" is not a kind of medicine but a type of livestock feed and so is the meal. I know from past experience, if you catch any of the day help at Allied Pill and Meal with a few dollars in his pocket, he cannot resist buying a few bundles of socks and maybe even putting a donation into the jug I set out with the sign on it reading HELP US PAY FOR EYE SURGERY.

I parked on the square, let down the back of my van, set up my table, and was setting out the jug when an old man, thin, gaunt and leathery, with a cheerfulness his appearance did not warrant, came up to me and said, "Pray for me, preacher! I'm eat up with the syph! I may have a son that's a rapiss, but I've got seven daughters and every one of them a beauty operator!" and then he walked on, greeting others he passed the same way.

We had been open for business about ten minutes when this character who had been sitting on a bench on the courthouse lawn came running over to greet me. I remembered him, then, as a talker, nonstop. He was a small person and had been a boxer and his ears were all battered into clumps and so were his brains. He was from up north and I cannot explain how he ever wound up in Arkansas, with his brains slapped to pulp, but there he was. He grabbed me and said, "Brother Edgar! What

1 9

you say there!!" I acted like I was glad to see him, I could not do anything else, and he said to me, out of the blue, "All I got for Christmas was a han' fulla saccharin tablets!"

He sat beside me the rest of the day, talking like that as I sold socks.

It was nearing the end of summer and I could tell lots of my customers were thinking ahead, buying three and four bundles of socks, having the sense enough to know that winter was coming, if not next week, at least before I could get back their way. I did not get my hands on any old gold that day but I did collect fifteen dollars in entrance fees to the poetry contest from three local residents, one of whom was the high school principal and who pointed out to me, in a confidential aside, that artificial sweeteners were unknown in the time of George Washington.

Late in the afternoon, as Morales was opening another bale of socks, all made out of the same type cotton material as a Turkish bath towel, and was placing them on the table, the boxer, whose name, so I would swear, was Kid Garlic, pulled me aside and said, "Brother Edgar, have I ever told you about the night I scroon an ardis mottel? You'd be innerested in how I done it, you being a holy man, and all." I had to sit there and listen to his story, something about him being hired by an ad agency in Little Rock to pose as a boxer with some girl in a swimming suit, who was about twenty and whose name was Bambi Jo Lustgarten, or so he said. I did not pay any attention to his story once I learned the girl's name since getting a Bambi Jo Lustgarten to yield to your advances represented no accomplishment.

At about three o'clock, Kid Garlic left, heading to his house, running and shadow boxing as he went and I got busy and retied the runners on a Japanese fly rod an old man named Lull Spivey had brought in that morning for me to repair.

I closed up at four o'clock. Morales and me were going to rent a room at the Slumber Nooky Lodge, the only one in town, and spend the night in Como, but first, I took most of the cash I had taken in that day to the post office and bought a money order with it. I asked the man behind the counter to fill it out for me, payable to The Little Brothers of St. Mortimer, and then I asked if he would mind selling me a stamped envelope and addressing it to The Little Brothers of St. Mortimer, P.O. Box 213, Benton, Arkansas.

This was all done deliberately. I did not want to have a lot of cash on me because the highways are crowded with bad men who would not hesitate to rob a poor "holy man" such as myself, and also it would get back to the people in town that I did send the money I made to "them brothers" I work for.

It also does me no harm in those parts to be thought unable to write, even to address an envelope. Once every six or eight weeks, I get to Benton, retrieve the money orders and bank them, then draw out the money with a check and invest it in certificates of deposit, utility stocks, real estate, and the like. I have been doing this for six years, banking around a hundred dollars a day, with the result that today I am, at least by my standards, as rich as cat milk.

At six o'clock, we went to supper. I parked the van behind Plumrod's Cafe and me and Morales went in the front door and Slovis Plumrod, himself, was there at the cash register and he greeted us. "How do, Brother Edgar," and he nodded at Morales. It makes a man feel good to be greeted by name in a place he has not visited in nearly a year but I should not make over much of it because we had been parked two blocks away, selling socks all day and in a town the size of Como, it would not have taken twenty minutes for everyone who lived there to know my name and business. On the other hand, it could be he remembered my name because I am a reputable merchant who will refund a buyer's money if he is dissatisfied, no matter how long ago I sold him the socks and this is well known and I have got a lot of advantage out of it.

It was crowded inside Plumrod's Cafe, most of the tables were filled and just about all the stools at the counter were taken. Above the fried foods and the coffee and the onions, and the chili, the room smelled of the aftershave lotions favored by men on parole.

Morales and me sat down at a table and a waitress brought us the menu. She was about four and a half feet tall, and had a lot of blond hair, worn in a lot of curls, like a pentecostal country music singer would wear hers. Her name, according to a pin on her dress, was Apple Lisa, and she looked ignorant, like she might want to do something bad to you if she found out you could read and write or knew what Wyoming was.

Last time we were in Plumrod's, Morales and me ordered Filet of Sea Trout à la Gookin, Gookin being Fern Gookin, who was Slovis Plumrod's girlfriend and who was in charge of the kitchen, and it was about the best piece of fish you will ever come across in an Arkansas town of three thousand people. Fern Gookin rolled it in Nabisco butter cookie crumbs then fried it in peanut oil. I mean to tell you, it was good, so I told Apple Lisa to bring us two Sea Trout à la Gookin and french fries and we sat back to wait for it. Morales never pays attention to much, but me, I always like to look over everybody I ever see, to try and figure out as much as I can about them. Four women were sitting at a table nearby and they were talking about some family in town that did not have any money, none at all, poor being just the word for them. "They live on *watt rah-ss*" one of the women said, which was her way of saying "white rice." Throughout this narrative, I will translate the dialect for you, if needed. Two men who were police of some kind, maybe city detectives, but probably sheriff's deputies in plain clothes, were sitting next to us and eating cream of kale soup, another house specialty. They were in plain clothes but I could tell what they were and so could Morales, by their polyester suits and their fat guts and their prescription sunglasses, and by their general look of being totally corrupt.

Slovis Plumrod came out from behind the cash register and walked around the room, stopping here and there to talk to his customers. When he got to our table, I asked him how he was doing. "Brother Edgar, I'm so down in the dumps, it would take a dog on far [fire] to make me laugh." I did not really want to hear about it, but he went on, about how the state restaurant inspectors were forcing him to put in a new grease trap or something and how it was going to cost him three thousand dollars to get it and how his Ford Gran Torino was not running smooth and he took it down to the shop and they had to put in a new carburetor because they found the old one clogged with human hair. Someone stepped up to the cash register to pay his check and Slovis got up from our table and headed over to take their money, turning to us as he left saying, "Enjoy your meal!" in a way that sounded like we would be in a lot of trouble if we did not.

Something, some sixth sense, made me look at Morales and I saw him stiff in his chair, like he was frozen and it seemed as if the life had drained out of him. Apple Lisa arrived about that time with our dinners and set them down. I wanted to start in on mine, I wanted to bring a big bite of that sea trout up off my plate with my fork but I could not eat with Morales in such a state. "What's the matter?" I asked him.

"Das Mariposa!" he whispered. There he was again, excited and lapsing into a combination of languages, this time, German and Spanish.

"A butterfly?" I asked him. "Where is it, in your salad?" and I looked down at his plate of lettuce and tomatoes half expecting to see some of the green moving its wings, although it would have been hard for a butterfly to move anything if he was covered with as much blue cheese salad dressing as was on the plate. Morales shook his head and nodded in the direction of a man who was sitting by himself at a table near the door, eating a hot dog, another house specialty.

"Mariposa," said Morales again, very much under his breath, and I looked at the man again, and saw what Morales was talking about, for he had a small butterfly tattooed on his left cheek.

Morales shivered. *"El Niño de Flumen Blanc!"* he whispered in terror. More of that damn language of his! I had to figure it out. *El niño*—the kid—*de*—of—*flumen*—river—*blanc* —white. The kid of the river white. *The White River Kid!* Here?

In Plumrod's Cafe? I looked at the man again. It was the White River Kid, all right. There could be no mistaking that butterfly tattooed on his face. The White River Kid was here in Como, eating supper like he was not being hunted by every law officer between Kansas City and New Orleans. There had been nothing but the White River Kid in the papers ever since he killed those six or eight people.

I looked at the Kid as close as I dared. The papers said he was twenty-five but he looked older and he was smaller than I had imagined him, he was almost tiny, no bigger than a jockey. He was not a handsome man and even had kind of a ratlike look about his face.

The two police officers, or deputies, whatever they were, sitting at the table next to us, spotted the White River Kid about the same time Morales did and started talking soft to each other, while trying not to look at him. I listened to them. They talked over what they had to do, there they were, officers of the law, and there was the Kid, a wanted man, they had to try to take him, it was their duty. They decided to walk up to the cashier, like nothing was wrong, pay their check, then go outside. One was going for help, the other was going to hide behind a car and shoot the White River Kid if he came through the door, shoot to kill him, with no two ways about it.

The two wiped their lips with paper napkins, picked up the check, and started for the counter where Slovis Plumrod was waiting to take their money, and they paid and left the building, to put their plan into operation.

I turned to Morales, who had heard everything I had, and said, "They mean to kill that boy, right while we're sitting here eating Filet of Sea Trout à la Gookin! We can't let them do that!"

Morales took a mouthful of sea trout and while still chewing it, said, *"Policia—les fleeks—ce merde!"* I gathered Morales was trying to tell me that police, in general, were treacherous and despicable, and I started in again, putting my position to him, namely, that I had a duty to try and save that boy's life, when he interrupted me. *"Chamaco—El Niño de Flumen Blanc—*

pistola. Summa pistola! In Hickock! Wait! we see *policia matado . . ."*

"Policia matado?" Morales was trying to tell me that the Kid had a big gun in his belt and if shooting started, maybe "the fleek," as he called the police, would get killed. When he saw that I understood what he had been saying, he took another mouthful of sea trout and smiled cynically.

Being locked up in Angola can made a man bitter when it comes to the police.

"I'm going to warn him!" I said to Morales. "I'm going to let him know there is a cop with a loaded gun waiting to kill him when he steps out the door." I started to get up but Morales put his hand on my arm and held me in the chair.

"El Niño—ragazzo—amore kill! *Septem, octo,* maybe, *decem,* dead. *Niño* not know you *amigo!* Not know you *bon vir!* Not *comprende!* You *matado*!"

Morales was trying to tell me the Kid would not understand what I was trying to do and probably take a few shots at me when I got near him. Morales might be right, but I just could not sit still and let that boy get killed right in front of my eyes, no matter what he had done, no matter how many people he had killed.

I got up and headed to the men's room. To get there I would have to pass the Kid's table. He saw me getting near him but kept on eating his hot dog. When I got right beside him, I knelt down like I was tying my shoe and said, "Kid, I am a friend. There is a cop waiting to kill you if you go out the front door. If you're smart, you'll go out the back way right now, slow and easy, and get away from here." I saw the Kid slowly reach his hand under the table and unbutton a blue jean jacket he was wearing and I saw he had a pistol stuck in his belt. I went on past him, into the men's room, stayed there awhile then came out. The Kid was gone. I went back to my table and sat down.

"Where did he go?" I asked Morales.

Morales said, "He got up and walked into the kitchen and that was the last I seen of him."

That went pretty easy, I thought. I got the Kid out of the

trap and if there was to be gunplay, it would be later, away from Plumrod's Cafe. Morales said something to me about being a brave man to go up to a killer like the White River Kid and talk to him and be so cool about it. I did not tell Morales then and there, but I have always been able to do what had to be done, no matter how terrifying it was. I thought back to the time in the army when I had to crouch down in a foxhole while an army tank ran its treads right over the top of the hole, which was some sort of training exercise to show us how safe it was in a foxhole, and I was able to do it with no show of fear but inside I was terrified because I have always had claustrophobia, and from boyhood on have had nightmares about being buried alive, which is what would have happened to me if that tank had stopped while on top of my foxhole.

Morales and me finished our supper, and even had a bowl of rice pudding, which Fern Gookin makes with honey and chopped pecans, and we lingered over coffee and then got up and left the cafe.

Outside, it was still light. There were some police officers there, maybe ten of them, with pump shotguns, and some automatic weapons, and they were obviously upset, milling around, tense as cats in heat. As Morales and me were about to get into our van, which was parked near the back of the cafe, one of the policemen came over to us and said, "Reverend, did you just come out of the cafe?" I said I did, and the policeman asked me if I had seen a young fellow inside, about twenty-five, wearing blue jeans and cowboy boots with a brass plate on the toe. I told him I had not noticed anyone like that. The policeman said he had a butterfly tattooed on his cheek. I turned to Morales and said, "Did you see anyone with a butterfly on his cheek?" Morales said he had not. I said I had not either and that I felt I was sure I would have noticed anything like that. The policeman said to be careful, Reverend, because we are talking about the White River Kid, who was seen inside there not a half hour ago but who has now disappeared. He is dangerous, said the policeman. I thanked him, then Morales and me got in the van and started out of the lot, planning to get a room down the highway, at the Slumber Nooky Lodge, where we had stayed about two years ago, and which was the one place in the whole county where you would find a halfway young hooker.

Morales was driving. He pulled out of the cafe parking lot and turned right on the highway, heading to the Slumber Nooky. We had not gone a hundred yards when there was a commotion in the back of the van, back where the socks are piled up in bundles, and then we heard a kind of dopey voice say, "We're back here, Reverend, hid in amongst these socks. Don't stop, just keep on going."

"Who is it talking?" I asked. There were a few seconds of silence, as Morales kept the van headed down the highway, then a stack of socks was pushed out of the way by someone down in behind it and I saw the face of the White River Kid.

"We know you are our friend," said the Kid. I heard him say "we." Who is the "we" he was talking about, I wondered. I did not want to ask, I did not want to press him and I did not have to, because just about that time, some more bundles of sox were pushed out of the way from behind and I saw that waitress, that Apple Lisa, from Plumrod's Cafe, the one who looked so dumb.

The White River Kid and Apple Lisa stood up and shook off the cramps they got being scrunched up under the socks. Then they came up to the front of the van and stood there behind me and Morales.

"You're the only man I ever met in all my life who has ever done anything to help me," said the Kid. He had his jacket buttoned up again, but there was no doubt he still had that pistol stuck in the top of his pants.

The Kid went on. "I woulda got kilt back yonder, if it wadn't for you. I went out the back like you said and I seen him, hiding behind a pickup, with a shotgun, just like you said, aimed at that cafe door." The Kid talked slow, like his mind was fogged, like he was half asleep. I do not think it was dope, I think it was brain damage from not getting enough of the right foods when he was young. "I was hiding back yonder and I heard you tell them police you had not seen me, I heard it through the wall. I would have been killed if it hadn't been for you." The Kid had a way of repeating himself, but I could stand listening to him.

"You are my friend," said the Kid. I breathed easier and could tell Morales was now a little more relaxed, but I could also see that I was already in a lot of trouble, aiding and abetting a wanted man escape from the law, for a start.

I figured the best thing to do was play up to the Kid and try to humor him until I could get rid of him, shake him off somehow, him and that dumb-looking Apple Lisa. "I'm proud to be your friend, Kid, proud to." I smiled and put out my hand to him.

He took it and said, "You're the first man to ever want to shake with me." This Kid was really socially deprived, I thought, if he has lived this long and no one has ever done him a favor or ever wanted to shake his hand. That may be true, but more likely, he is just one of those mental cases that thinks people treat him wrong, some kind of persecution complex, probably.

The Kid noticed Apple Lisa standing there beside him and said, "This is my girl," and I said, pleased to meet you and so did Morales because we sure did not want to rub the Kid the wrong way. "This is my girl," he repeated, "and we're going to her house, so I can meet her people. We're fixing to get married and she wants me to meet her people first."

"Congratulations!" I said to the Kid, still trying to humor him. "Congratulations and may you have all the happiness in the world."

The Kid smiled at me, the first time, and said, "She's gonna get me a job helping her daddy."

"Wonderful, Kid," I said. "Where is her house? Somewhere around here? We'll be glad to drop you off. Whereabouts she live?"

"Whereabouts is it?" the Kid asked Apple Lisa.

"Block Island," said Apple Lisa. Block Island was way down in the southern part of the state, maybe three hundred miles away.

I asked, "How you planning to get there, Kid? You need bus

fare? I'll be glad to buy your tickets! It'll be my wedding present."

The Kid shook his head. "Don't want bus tickets," he said.

"Then how you plan to get there?" I asked.

The Kid smiled again, and said, "You're going to take us, you and that Spic at the wheel!"

THREE

So there we were, on the way to Block Island, three hundred miles away, and it turns out that Apple Lisa's family does not actually live in Block Island, but outside of it about a mile, so far outside of it that it is probably not even still in Arkansas, but into Texas. I asked her, is it Texas or is it Arkansas. She said, "Some say it is Texas, some say it is Arkansas. It has never been one way or the other to me," which proved that she was as dumb as she looked, as if it needed to be proved, as if any girl with even half her marbles would have ever even got mixed up with the White River Kid, much less be planning to marry him.

Morales was driving. I could tell he was thinking black thoughts, about me and how my act of charity had backfired on us, and about the Kid and what he was going to have to do in the end to get rid of him.

Apple Lisa and the White River Kid were in one of the bunks in back of the van, making love. "Fucking," they called it. Morales would not even speak to me, he was so mad at me, so I had no one to talk to, and I started going over things in my mind. For one thing, I could not stop in towns and set up shop and sell any more socks until I had got rid of the Kid and his girlfriend. That would cost me plenty, for it was still summer and there were lots of folks in those little towns on pretty days and I was going to miss out on at least a hundred dollars tax free every day I had the Kid on my neck.

I tried to remember what I had read in the papers about the Kid but it was not much. I did not pay any special attention to the stories about him, to me he was just another crazy killer who goes on a binge, the sort that you can read about somewhere in this country any time you pick up a paper. I recalled that he got his name, the White River Kid, because he grew up along it, between DeValls Bluff, Arkansas, and Forrest City and first got in trouble when he was real young and got caught stealing catfish off a trot line set in the White River. Except for that, I could not remember much, nothing about who he had killed or when or why.

Whatever, else, I was in big trouble, both me and Morales, because every mile we went, we were taking him farther and farther away from the law that was looking for him, we were harboring a fugitive and abetting his escape. Probably we would get into it for transporting that Apple Lisa, who now looked to be about sixteen maybe younger, and if we crossed a state line, they would end up slapping me with the Mann Act, even though there was nothing of that sort to it.

I looked back to where the Kid and Apple Lisa were, on the bunk, now both passed out and sleeping, both as naked as jaybirds, just animals, the both of them.

There are no guns hidden in the van, nothing to throw down on the Kid with, no knives, except the long, sharp one Morales carries in his boot, no hammers or tire irons to bend around the Kid's head.

Morales saw the Kid was asleep with the girl beside him, both of them naked in the bunk, naked, right in the same van with me and Morales. The sight turned Morales on, but not me, not like it would once have. Time was, the sight of a young couple naked in a bed would have made me get up one of those old-time wedding-night hards, one where the head of your pecker just saucers out, but those days were gone.

If ever Morales and me were going to do anything to take the Kid, now would have been the time. His pistol was lying there on the floor of the van, almost kicked under his bunk and he was out cold. Now would be the time, and Morales wanted to take advantage of it. "Let's kill heem, heem and the girl, too!" he whispered to me as I sat beside him in the front of the van. "I weel do eet! Eet is no problem!"

"We can't kill anyone, Morales!" I whispered back. "We're already in a lot of hot water as it is. Killing them is not the way. I know we've got to get rid of them, right enough, and we may have to kill them before it's over, but we can't do it right now, in the van. We've got to get rid of them in some way so the Kid won't be able to say I helped him escape, that's the important part. Sure, I could stop the first time we see a state trooper and jump out and start screaming 'Save us! Save us!' to him, but it would not work unless we could see to it that the Kid and the girl were both killed by the law, right then and there, before either one of them could say the first word about our part in this. Right now, it looks like the easiest thing to do is to drive them on down to Block Island, or beyond, put them off at her folks' house and then just wave a peaceable good-bye to them. So far, nobody's seen us with them, Lord let's hope not, that tattoo on his face is like a neon sign, telling people, Here I Am, the White River Kid, wanted for killing six or eight! Call the Law to come get me and all them I'm with!"

I could tell Morales was disgusted and I could not be sure he would not slip back there while the Kid was asleep and put that knife of his in his heart and the girl's too. Morales said he was tired and he wanted me to drive so he could sleep. Morales had his heart set on getting that room in Como, at the Slumber Nooky Lodge, because they show adult movies in the rooms and he loves to watch them. They are adult and not X-rated, it being in Arkansas, and we should be thankful for what we can get, but I do not find adult movies interesting, all that simulation. To me adult movies are nothing but diet porn and cannot hold a candle to the real thing.

Morales stopped the van and got out of the driver's seat and I took over the wheel and we started off again, driving along some Arkansas back road in the sheer darkness, the van's headlights just opening a glimpse of the road, just enough for me to see when to turn, when to slow down. Morales went back to his bunk, right across the aisle from where the White River Kid and Apple Lisa were lying, naked.

I was alone, thinking my own thoughts, cursing myself for committing an act of Christian charity that had ended by having me held hostage by an unknown quantity like the White River Kid, when he silently sat down in the seat next to me. He had pulled on his pants, worn blue jeans that were out at the knees, and had the pistol stuck in the top of them. He had on no shirt and no shoes. I hate being slipped up on and have always wanted to have a big dog, with good ears, around me at all times to prevent people from getting near me without my knowing it. A rottweiler would be good for this, I understand they are the most dog for the money, but I have never even seen one, to my knowledge, and would not know where to buy one, and probably would not be happy with a dog, anyway, after I had him, for I am a man who does not want responsibility, I do not want to have to feed a dog or clean up after him, so I will probably go through life being slipped up on for this reason.

Even though he had slipped up on me, and even though I knew his reputation from the newspapers, for some reason I was not afraid of the White River Kid. He was a killer, I had no doubt of it, he carried a gun, there it was, stuck right in the top of his pants, and I had no doubts he would just as soon pull it out and empty it into a stranger as look at him, but for some reason, I was not afraid of him and neither was Morales, if I am any judge, and I am. When you have tossed around as much as I have, when you have rubbed shoulders with as many different types of people as I have, starting in the army, well, even starting as far back as the first grade in Romeo, Texas, going on through all the people I have met in all the jobs I have had, you might say that I can read a man, that I can predict what he will do as well as, or better than, the next fellow. Because of this, I was not worried about the White River Kid killing us, me and Morales, although I would not want to go so far as to say he might not want to one day get rid of that waitress, Apple Lisa, who might turn out to be even too dumb to please the White River Kid.

The Kid rode beside me at least five miles, before he said a word, then he spoke. "Ain't nobody before you ever done me any favors." There was more silence, then he asked, "You got any kids?" It was then I knew I had him. I have observed ever since I got up past forty or forty-five, that there are a world of young men floating around, most of them in trouble of one kind or another, who are looking for somebody to be a father to them, some older man to guide them. I have had it happen to me many times in the past, partly, I guess because of the role I play on the road, that of a Brother of some kind, and I appear to be a ready-made father to these people. There are so many young men looking for fathers and I am convinced it is because so many real fathers are not worth a damn, with no idea of what being a father is all about. I have a born gift for being a father, and all it is an understanding of what it takes, and that is, consistency and encouragement. I recommend to any man who is about to become a father to train himself to be consistent and be encouraging. I have never been a real father myself, never having been married, and lucky in other ways as well, but I have come near to being a father once or twice.

The first time, was when I was living in New Orleans, right after I got back to the United States after working as the ship's doctor. I lived there three years, working as a waiter at Trout's Pie Shop, a coffeehouse in the French Quarter. Coffeehouses were big in those days and I had this great friend then, a man from Arlington, Virginia, named Muir Appleblossom. His parents were English and he spoke with an English accent which made it possible for him to get away with a name like he had, Muir Appleblossom, without being harassed all the time. Muir was a desk clerk at the Dodge Hotel, in the Quarter, owned back then by an old Jew man named Mischa Feinstein, and me and Muir used to screw this nurse at DePaul Hospital, a girl about twenty-three, named Saraha Stafford. She had two rows of teeth in the front of her mouth, it did not cause any problem, and she did not look deformed, it was just a fluke, a trick of the genes, or something. Anyway, me and Muir and Saraha used to get together three or more afternoons a week in a room at the Dodge Hotel for three-ways. This went on about a year, more fun than you can imagine, and we were all three happy with everything we had and everything we did. Then one day, Saraha turned up pregnant, and it was either me or Muir that was responsible. She wanted to have an abortion but in those days, you could not just go into an office and announce you wanted an abortion and get it, and have it even covered by your health and accident policy.

So we were all three in a kind of nervous state there for a while, until Muir got the idea of bringing Dr. Botto into the picture. Dr. Solon Botto was a man about fifty, too fat, and with no chin, who was a surgeon at DePaul Hospital, which was about three blocks from the Dodge Hotel. He used to check in, with Muir on the desk, about once a week for a little afternoon quickie with a girl who was living with Blitz Pompano, the football player, at the time, but who used to get with Dr. Botto once in a while because he would give her drugs, which she passed on to Blitz, who needed them because his knees were always out of whack, and you could bend them either way. I have always said you should not be able to call a man a professional athlete until he learns how to drain the fluid off his own knees. Muir got the idea of introducing Saraha to Dr. Botto and letting him get a little action, and then after a while, she would tell the doctor she was pregnant and he would surely take care of the abortion. Well, that is exactly what happened, Muir stopped the doctor the next afternoon, as he was registering, and said, "Doc, I've got a friend who has been dying to meet you," and it went from there. Saraha had a few afternoons with him in the Dodge Hotel, then told him she was pregnant, and the doctor —have I said yet that he was not too bright?—had her into his office one afternoon, on a day when the office was closed, it was just Saraha and the doctor, and he performed an abortion and that was the end of it, and that was one of the times I nearly became a father.

So there was the White River Kid, sitting next to me in a van moving through the night, wearing nothing but a pair of ragged blue jeans, with a chest no bigger than a twelve year old boy's, lonely, wondering what was going to happen to him, too limited by his upbringing to be able to take hold of his life and do something with it, scared, probably, and looking for a father to talk to.

If there is one thing I have learned these lonely boys want to talk to a father about it is sexual triumphs, and feeling sure of that, I jumped right into it with the White River Kid.

"That girl back there," I said, nodding in the direction of Apple Lisa, "you got her knocked up?"

The Kid shook his head then said, "I don't know."

"You gotta be careful, Kid," I said. "If you don't, you'll always have little babies around, crying and wanting you to feed them."

The mention of babies made the Kid think of his own childhood in a shanty on the banks of the White River. "It was drinking wine made my momma have babies. She'd drink that wine ever night, drink it with Lucky or Junior, and 'fore long, she'd have another baby. They was eight of us. One day, Miss Jeannie come to th' house and took us all away, and put us with other people, in some kind of care."

"Foster care?" I asked.

"That was it," said the Kid, "foster care!"

That explains everything as far as the Kid's being out of step with society was concerned. I have never known a drunk, a criminal, a crazy of any kind who had not been taken from his family and put in foster care when he was young. The Kid went on to tell me he was put in a foster home in DeWitt, Arkansas, with a couple that were Holiness and as soon as they had him in their care, they took him down to some tabernacle and got him baptized in a pond on the grounds. Every night, they whipped his ass to drive out the devil, and the Kid had no background to draw on to know they were the crazy ones, not him. The damage that foster care does to children is bigger than the damage that would be done to them if they were left to live with their family, even though the family had to struggle just to keep from starving, but this is a notion ahead of its time.

As I talked to the Kid, I got to feel altogether different toward him. He seemed to like talking to me, too, and although he did not speak the language all that perfectly, it was possible to follow his talk with no trouble.

I started to try and find out what I could. "Kid, the papers are full of stories about you. They true?"

"What kind of stories?" he asked.

"They say, for instance, you used to take catfish off of other people's trot lines in the White River."

The Kid laughed. "Yeah," he said. The mention of fish started a line of thought and he asked, "You ever seen a big gar? One really big?" He held out as far as his arms would reach. "Six feet long, sometimes, seven!" he said. I had seen such gar, I said, and in fact had a relative, Uncle Willis Nail, who used to go on float trips on the White River, using deep sea tackle to catch gar and who came into town once with a six-foot gar strapped across the front bumper of his 1946 Ford.

"They's mean," he said, "they ain't nothing meaner than a gar. They can take your hand off, with them jaws of theirs." I could see the Kid's face brighten. "You know what I like to do?"

"What's that, Kid?"

"Lay out one of them big, long, dead gar on his side and take a great old big ax and raise it back over my head and bring it down on his side."

"Why's that, Kid?"

"Sparks! 'Cause the sparks'll fly!"

"You mean, gar is so tough, hitting them with an ax will make the sparks?"

"Sure," said the Kid, smiling, looking off.

That poor White River Kid. He must be the most socially and culturally deprived person I have ever met. Here I am, talking like a social worker. One time, when I was in a doctor's office, or maybe it was a government office, I was in the waiting room, nothing to do and I picked up a professional social workers' journal. *Social Work*, I think that was the name of it. I thumbed through it, trying to read some of the articles, but they were written in a kind of way that my mind would not take hold, it just kept slipping off. It was the style, I guess, the jargon, the long, wordy paragraphs. Finally, I managed to get into one of the articles and was actually able to read it, some woman writing about electrically induced stress in welfare clients, or something like that, and every once in a while, she would throw in a line, "As Lincoln said in commenting on stress," or "recalling Lincoln's dictum, that the means test should be flexible . . ." Lincoln? I knew Abraham Lincoln had never lowered himself to pronounce on the principles of social work! What was this woman writer up to? She went on, Lincoln this, Lincoln that. I hung to the end, hoping to find out why she kept quoting Lincoln, no first name, just Lincoln. At the end, I made out what it was all about, she was not quoting Abraham Lincoln, I doubt, in fact, if she had ever heard of him. The one she was quoting was some other social worker, some woman named Rosalie Lincoln, who I gather was an authority in that murky world.

Anyway, even if it sounds like a social worker babbling, I am going to go ahead and say it, it looked to me like the White River Kid must have been about the most culturally deprived fellow I had ever run into. Instead of doing what other boys his age were doing, pitching horseshoes, playing softball, going to carnivals, riding the rides, he did nothing but go down to the riverbank and hit a dead gar on the side to make sparks. It is a sure thing he never went to school much beyond the sixth grade if that far and I know he was never a Boy Scout, or maybe never even heard of them, and I am sure he never played on any county school basketball team or baseball team. It would not be too farfetched to guess that he had never held a book in his hands, after the second grade. The only thing he was ahead of other boys his age in was the screwing department. I could tell by the way he was giving that Apple Lisa a good time that he was no green hand at it, and while he may never have seen a stage show, I do not think it mattered to him, as long as he had something close by to screw.

"What else they say, them papers?" asked the Kid.

I was going to throw the Kid the big question and I felt I had judged him well enough to be safe doing it. "They say you killed six or eight people. That true?"

The Kid's smile vanished, his face took on an altogether different look, sort of like the face of Harry Langdon, the silent movie comedian, the one that critic said had the "face of a baby dope fiend." The Kid spoke. "I ain't never killed any people," he said.

"Never?" I asked, taking my eyes off the road to look in his face.

He shook his head. "Never." I felt better about the Kid, really positive toward him. The papers were trying to lynch him. "I ain't never killed any people," the Kid repeated. I nodded my head and smiled at him. "Them things I killed, they wadn't people." I turned to look at him again, and I know my brow must have been wrinkled. "Them things I killed was not people, they was nothing but wooly gums."

"Wooly gums?" I asked. "What's wooly gums?" I thought the Kid might have in mind some kind of swamp creature, something that grows in the backwater along the White River, something like mud puppies or crawdads.

"Wooly gums is some kind of haint, some kind of thing like fog, only it's alive," he said.

"I don't understand, Kid."

"It's some kind of thing that can make itself look like people. They look like people, but they ain't, they're some kind of gas, trapped, and they can't get out unless they's dead, unless somebody kills them."

The Kid was insane! "How can you tell a wooly gum from a real person?" I asked, getting worried. "How do you know when something that looks like a person is not a person, but a wooly gum?"

The Kid answered me confidently. "The eyes," he said. "I can tell by the eyes."

"The eyes, Kid? How's that? What do you mean, the eyes?" Suddenly, I felt it important not to let the Kid see my eyes. I knew I was not a wooly gum, whatever that was, but who knows what I would look like to the White River Kid, who can say what he would find in my eyes.

"A wooly gum's eyes are different," he said. "Wooly gum's eyes got no light in them."

There was no doubt, the White River Kid was insane, totally, quietly mad, and any lawyer, even a public defender, ought to be able to keep him out of the electric chair if he ever got to trial for killing those six or eight. I recall the time in a town near Oxford, Mississippi, three or four years ago, when I was down there selling socks to beat the daylights, I heard two poor white boys talking outside the courthouse. One had been tried for something and had been convicted and had got three years and was out, waiting to see if he would get probation. The other one asked him if he had a lawyer when he went before the judge and he said, "No, I didn't have no lawyer. I had a public defender!"

Even a public defender could get the White River Kid off with a few years in the State Mental Hospital in Little Rock. All he would have to do is put him on the witness stand and get him to start talking.

"You know what I mean?" the Kid asked me. "About wooly gums? It ain't no crime to kill them, they ain't real people. They ain't nothing but haints and the shurrff won't care if you kill them all."

I thought it was time to get the Kid's mind off killing wooly gums, and chopping at dead gar with sharp axes, and looking for people with no light in their eyes, and I planned to ask him about that tattoo on his left cheek. It was a beauty, a genuine masterpiece of the tattooer's art, a true thing of beauty. If it had been done on something besides a human face, it would be displayed in an art gallery. It was like no butterfly I had ever seen in real life, being too feathery, too graceful, too ethereal to last ten minutes in the real world, if it were alive. And the colors, pinks, greens, rose, and purple, were unlike anything I had ever seen.

"Where did you get that butterfly on your cheek?" I asked him. He touched it with his right fingertips, brushing the spot where it was, gently, softly, sort of like he was stroking the butterfly.

"Is it still there?" he asked.

Still there? I thought to myself. Does he not know it is permanent? "It's still there, Kid, and a real beauty it is! Whereabouts you get it? Who did it?"

"Down home," he said.

"Where is home, Kid?"

The Kid shook his head. "I don't know."

"Where was home, where did it used to be when you got that butterfly put on your face?"

"Home? Along the river. The White River. No regular place."

That almost made me cry, stark, raving nuts though he might be, it was a sad thing to think of, a woman, drunk most of the time, eight kids, no money, no possessions, living here and there, in this shanty and that one, until some sheriff came and ran them out and they would move on to some other place.

"Do you remember who it was that did that tattoo?"

"Who was it? I remember. It was Bill."

Bill. That is all that the Kid remembered. "Who was Bill?" I asked.

"Bill? He was simple. He didn't have no sense. Somebody had to mind him all the time. He couldn't do nothing but draw butterflies on people."

This lost artisan, a simpleton, an idiot savant, maybe, like that man you see on television once in a while, some fellow who looks like the ape man, dressed up in a tuxedo, with an idiot's face on the head sticking out of his collar, who is led in to a room where the king of Sweden is sitting with all his retinue and this ape man is led to a piano and he is helped onto the bench, then he reaches out to the keyboard and plays something you recognize, something by Rachmaninoff, all the way through, a little rough but better than most people with good sense who have studied the piece for years.

"That butterfly makes you a marked man, Kid," I said. "Anyone that ever sets eyes on you knows that you are the White River Kid because all those stories about you in the papers always say the Kid has a butterfly tattooed on his cheek." The Kid touched his face again. "How long you had it?" I asked.

"Had what?" asked the Kid.

"That butterfly on your face?"

The Kid shook his head. "I can't keep too good a track of things like that. Maybe a long time. Two years. Maybe longer, maybe six weeks."

About that time Apple Lisa called to him from the bunk in the back, "Kid, come back here, right now! I want some more of what you got!"

"Apple Lisa's calling you, Kid."

"Apple what?" he said.

"Apple Lisa. That's her name," I said.

"Apple Lisa? Like in apples that you can buy and eat?"

"The same," I said.

The Kid shook his head from side to side. "I ain't never heard of no girl named Apple!"

It was obvious to me that the White River Kid did not know the name of the girl he had been screwing in the back of my van, not an hour earlier. "How long have you known her?" I asked.

"Know her?" he asked. "I don't know her at all. I never set eyes on her before in my life till she followered me out the back door of that cafe back yonder, the one where you kep them shurrffs from killing me cold."

"Come on back, Kid, I want some more!" yelled Apple Lisa. The Kid got up, walked back to the lower bunk where she lay, dropped his jeans and got on top of her. Morales Pittman was asleep in the lower bunk across the narrow aisle from them, but he did not wake up. When you have been in prison like Morales has, you get used to sleeping soundly even when two people in the next bunk are screwing like minks in heat.

FOUR

f I had not put my nose in where it did not belong, if I
had not tried to be a Christian, if I had not tried to
practice the commandment of Love Thy Neighbor as
Thyself, in other words, if I had sat by and let that deputy
sheriff in Como, Arkansas, shoot down the White River Kid as
he came out the front door of Slovis Plumrod's Cafe, his belly
full of hot dog, at that, I would be in bed right now in the
Slumber Nooky Lodge, not even thinking about getting up for
at least another three hours, and when I did, there would not be
any crazy man lurking around me, a pistol tucked in his drawers, and as soon ready to use it on me as look at me.

But no, I stepped in, lied to the law in the bargain, got myself
mixed up in helping a killer escape, and now here I was, driving
south at five-thirty in the morning, hungry, head aching, up all
night and sure as hell that there was going to be gun play
before it was over.

Up all night! I cannot remember the last time I was up all
night. I do not think I have ever been up all night, but I can
remember the last time I was awake this time of day. It was

about thirty years ago, when I was a lot younger and more able to take such things. I was in Florida, St. Augustine, with Bill Tuckahoe of Tuckahoe, Texas, him and some gambler friend of his they called Sportfish. Bill and Sportfish got the idea of getting up before the sunrise and going down to the pier and be fishing when it got daylight.

We got out on that fishing pier in the pitch dark, intending to fish, but the wind was so high, the waves were washing up over the end of it, and there was even a boat, a new, pretty cabin cruiser, thrown up on the beach, right there at the pier, and the water where we intended to fish was churning with huge sharks, crazy acting, flapping around, striking the underpinnings. I never knew what drew them all into that one spot, but there were more than I could sort out, thrashing, snapping at each other, and scaring the hell out of me. I wanted to get away from that pier, I was afraid all that commotion underneath it would push it over and there we would be, thrown in amongst that pack of devils. Bill Tuckahoe, he was terrified by the sharks and the wind and the waves, along with me and Sportfish, but he could not bring himself to leave the pier. He said afterward, it was horrible, but beautiful, too, and I guess in a way you could say that, especially since it was not long before the sun started coming up, out to sea, and directly it got lighter and lighter and the sea got calm and the sharks settled down and we could have tried to fish, if we had still wanted to, but by then we were all three hungry and went on back to the hotel, where we had pancakes and sausage and lots of orange juice.

Bill Tuckahoe was a lawyer at that time, but it was not long after they took away his license. He got disbarred for failure to thrive. The bar association said he was setting a bad example for the other lawyers in the state.

That same sun was coming up again, this time on my left, as I headed down the highway toward Block Island, where Apple Lisa's people lived, or so she said. They were still asleep in the same bunk, Apple Lisa and the White River Kid. Morales, he too was still asleep, but he was dressed, whereas, Apple Lisa and the Kid were stark naked. Funny, the sight did not excite me in any way. I guess I was too tired. I am nearly sixty years old and, they say, overweight, and I really should not have to experience the things I had gone through since late afternoon yesterday.

The Kid was crazy, that much was certain, crazy, but with kind of a big dog affection for me, or so I made out. I did not think he would be a danger to me, I did not think he would look in my eyes and see evidence that I was just a wooly gum, begging to be released by death. Still, I planned to keep my sunglasses on until I had got rid of the Kid, and I was going to warn Morales to do the same, as soon as I could.

Get rid of the Kid. How do they put it? "A consummation devoutly to be wished"? Somewhere along the line, they would get him, the sheriff's deputies or the highway patrol, and if they did not kill him, out-and-out right there, he would go right to the insane asylum. They would not execute him, like they would the same man who kills someone while pulling off a stickup or something like that. I have never agreed with the notion that we will not put a man to death if he is crazy, no matter what he has done. I know that is at the bottom of the English Common Law and all the statutes in the books, but it makes no sense to me. If there is anyone we are going to execute, it ought to be the crazy ones who will always be crazy and who will always be a menace to the rest of us unless they are kept under lock and key. It does not make sense to me to kill a man who murders his wife in a fit of rage, but to put up a true nut in comfort in the mental hospital for a few years then turn him loose if he promises to keep taking pills which will control his desire to kill. And another thing about punishing murder, we ought to be looking at the history of the one who gets killed. It could be that the murderer has done society a favor by getting rid of a rotten son of a bitch, some bully who has done nothing all his life but make things miserable for the rest of us. What about the worthless drunk who steals his wife's paycheck year after year and throws it away on booze? What about the son of a bitch who keeps beating up his wife and children? Has not the man who gets him off the earth done the rest of us a favor?

But I had other more important things on my mind than reforming the legal system. With this White River Kid taking over like he had, I was faced with the loss of income from selling socks. I could not stop wherever I pleased and set up shop, I was not even on my regular route, but was far off it, in towns I had not visited in years and where I did not have contacts, or know who to grease, if I had to. Furthermore, I was in an area where I did not know the location of the whorehouses or where to meet the fancy ladies who would work just for the fun of it.

One good thing, I was not likely to run out of money. I have told you earlier that I always mail the day's take home to the Little Brothers of St. Mortimer from the post office in whatever town I stop in. That is true, but I have not told you about the cash I keep in the van. I have two funds, one, about a thousand dollars in cold cash, which I keep locked in a drawer, which I use for buying old gold from poor widow women along the road, if I cannot get my hands on it any other way.

I also have another five thousand dollars in cash, all in twenty dollar bills, hidden in five different places in the van, secret, watertight boxes which I had welded in when I first started on the road. I keep that much money because you can never tell what trouble you might get in traveling across the south. There are a world of pitfalls awaiting the unsophisticated traveler, especially one like me, who once in a while might get involved with some child under age, or want to hire some farm girl to tan my ass with a cowhide. If things go wrong in a case like that, the best thing to have is a lot of cash money, ready at hand. Five thousand is really not enough, it ought to be twenty-five thousand, and I might just put that much on board, if I live to get back home. I have the five thousand dollars split up into five hiding places, because, if I ever had to pay off some law enforcement officer inside my van, I do not want to have to open a drawer and let him see five thousand when I have just told him all I have is one thousand. I also have another locked, watertight steel box welded under one of the bunks, where I keep the gold and jewelry I pick up during a run. So, if money was what it was going to take to get me out of this mess with the White River Kid, I had it at hand.

My thoughts were disturbed by Morales Pittman, tapping me on the shoulder. "They are hungry," he said, pointing to Apple Lisa and the White River Kid, who were dressed, and standing beside him. How could three people have got up out of bed and got dressed ten feet away from me without my hearing them? Impacted cerumen, I would guess, and I made a note to go by the clinic if I got home and have both my ears flushed.

We were all tired and hungry, right enough. "We should stop at a motel and all get cleaned up," said Morales.

"And let's get something to eat, too," said Apple Lisa, twisting her leg around one of the Kid's legs. I knew neither Apple Lisa or the Kid would have any money, that whatever we spent until we could get rid of them was going to come out of my pocket, but I did not object, I even welcomed the chance to let the Kid see me doing him a favor, but I had taken the precaution of taking a few bills out of my wallet and putting them in my pants pocket, so that Kid would not see any twenties and take a notion to kill me for them.

"It's time to stop and get some breakfast," I said to the three of them. "As soon as I see a place, I'll pull over." I noticed the Kid smile and Apple Lisa actually jumped up and down. Seeing him smile, I thought it was a good time to take up the matter of that butterfly on his face, and I pulled the van off the road, stopped, and turned off the engine.

"Kid, we've got to do something about that butterfly if we are going to go in a restaurant. We've got to cover it up." The Kid did not comprehend, damn his thick head. I had to explain to him that every peace officer in the country was looking for a slight-built kid with a butterfly tattooed on his cheek and that if one saw him, he would start shooting first and ask questions afterward. I finally got it across to the Kid that I was going to have to put a Band-Aid over the butterfly, and when he agreed I went to the little first aid kit I carry and brought out some

Band-Aids and put one of them across the butterfly. I noticed that the Kid had no beard, no whiskers had grown during the night, his cheek was as smooth as it must have been when he was ten years old. "Don't you shave?" I asked him.

He shook his head. "Don't need to."

After I had covered up the butterfly, I took another Band-Aid and put it across an imaginary cut on his forehead, and a second on his chin.

"What's them extra ones for?" he asked. "They's just one butterfly!"

"Camouflage, Kid, camouflage!" I said. I might as well have tried to explain in Russian, for all he understood about camouflage. I put it another way. "To throw the police off! A deputy sheriff seeing one Band-Aid across your face where the butterfly is might just figure out that you got it there to hide something, but let him see bandages all over your face, and he won't think a damn thing about butterflies! Just leave it to me, Kid. If anybody asks what those bandages are for, just let me do the talking." The Kid said he would and I hoped he understood and would do as he said. I could see Morales smiling at me, appreciating my good sense about the camouflage.

We started out again and before long, I saw a Waffle Shoppe along the highway and we pulled off the road and into the parking lot. I looked inside, there was no one there, no customers, that is, only the counterman, so I said to them, let's go inside and get a good breakfast and I told the White River Kid and Apple Lisa to order anything they wanted and that it would be my treat.

As soon as we were in the door and making our way to seats at a table, the counterman saw the Kid, saw the bandages on his face. "What happened to you, fella, did you get jumped by a timber wolf?"

The Kid looked to me for guidance and I said, right away, to the counterman, "Skin cancer! His face is eat up with them!" That shut the counterman up and he took down our order. Apple Lisa ordered french fries and a large Coke, that was all. I urged her to order something more traditional, at least toast and jelly and maybe an order of bacon, but it did no good. She stuck to french fries and a large Coke. The Kid studied the menu awhile, looked puzzled by it, looked embarrassed, as embarrassed as is possible for a killer of six or eight to look, and I realized he could not read, so I asked him, "How about some hotcakes and syrup and some sausage?" and he said yes.

The counterman knew his business. You might even say, as countermen go, he was an artist. He threw the sausage and bacon and the slice of country ham Morales ordered on the grill first, then he started frying the eggs and the potatoes next, and then he turned the ham and the bacon and the sausage and put the bread in the toaster with one hand and with the other he poured the hotcake batter on the griddle, and before long he was moving behind that counter like one of those variety acts that balances a dinner plate on a thin pole and starts it to twirling while he balances another. In the end, he had it all ready at the same time and served it all at once. What he was able to do for four breakfasts was probably nothing to what he would have to do when the rush came along, about seven-thirty or eight o'clock. It is a shame that people like him, men who can do something really well, hardly ever get recognized for it.

The food was well prepared and we all enjoyed it, all that is, except Apple Lisa, who nibbled one of the french fries and sipped a little of the Coke, then put her head down on the table and fell asleep. There was something wrong with that girl, something in her brain that would not allow her to operate all the time on full power. I wonder what kind of job she did waiting table at Slovis Plumrod's cafe. The chances are she did a poor job, and I would guess Plumrod kept her around more for her skill when granting sexual favors, and from what I had observed between her and the Kid, I would say she could suck the chrome off a trailer hitch, than her ability to wait table.

We lingered in the Waffle Shoppe. It was still too early for any other customers, and we sat there at the table, me, Morales, and the Kid drinking coffee, and Apple Lisa snoring away. I had the feeling that we were sort of a family, making a trip together, and I am sure the counterman, if he was to be questioned by any lawmen, would have said, "They looked like a father, that'd be the fat old man with the rope full of knots around his belly; his son and daughter-in-law (that would be the Kid and Apple Lisa); and some kind of Mexican. It may have been a father, his daughter and her husband, that would be the Mexican, and another son, him with the face eat up by cancer. That's more like it! That's what it must have been, the daughter married to the Mexican. But, now, it could of been, an old man, his two children and some Mexican they picked up hitchhiking. Damn, that scares me! Them picking up a hitchhiker!"

When I paid for the breakfasts, I left the counterman a five dollar tip. That was in part because I wanted to acknowledge his skill at his business, but also because I wanted him to remember us, because as I put away my change, I said, "Yes sir, skin cancer! Got it bad! That's why we're taking him to Houston, to that big clinic." I leaned close to the man, and said, in an undertone, "It's so bad, they're going to have to surgically remove his whole face and replace it with one carved out of Lucite and anchored to his skull with solid gold bolts! I'm telling you, his momma's taking it hard!"

Once we were all back in the van and heading south again, I noticed the Kid relax and actually smile once or twice. All the time we had been in the Waffle Shoppe, he had kept his hand on the handle of that pistol tucked in his pants, and I am sure he would have started blazing away with it if he had taken the notion the counterman, or even me or Morales or Apple Lisa was another wooly gum, some collection of vapor formed to look like a person, but really a spirit, a spook, hoping someone would kill it and give it release.

We were near Texarkana, Arkansas, which is on the border between Arkansas and Texas. That part of town on the Texas side is Texarkana, Texas, and there are some beer joints there that straddle the line, half in Texas and half in Arkansas, with a white line painted down the middle of the floor. Block Island, where Apple Lisa's people lived, was in the vicinity, and we would soon be there.

I had been driving all night while Morales slept. I was tired and could go no farther. I told the Kid and Apple Lisa I would get them a room so they could rest and get cleaned up before the Kid met her parents. Morales looked at me with pure disgust in his face but the Kid and Apple Lisa thought it was a good idea. Morales did not know about the five thousand dollars I had hidden in the van. All he knew about was the place where I hid the rings and other gold I picked up along the way. While I trusted Morales, still, I see no point in telling anyone everything about yourself.

I told Morales I had enough money to handle it, enough to get two rooms, so he gave up his objections. In fact, I could see it dawning on him that I had a good idea, to get the Kid and Apple Lisa in a room by themselves, and then from our room, call the sheriff and tell him where he could find the White River Kid and then slip away in time so we would not have to witness the gun battle. Morales even gave me a wink, to let me know he saw what I had in mind and thought it was a good idea.

There was a Ramada Inn in Texarkana and that is where I headed. I went in to the desk and registered. I was in a vehicle with The Little Brothers of St. Mortimer painted on the sides of it, so I had to put my real name down on the card. I registered as "Brother Edgar" and "Missionary party" and was given two rooms. I paid in cash, after requesting and being given the sales tax exemption and the usual discount rate for religious activities.

The two rooms were next to each other, on the ground floor, in the back. I parked the van, locked it up tight, and showed the Kid and Apple Lisa into one of the rooms. "This is yours, Kid," I said, and I could see he was overwhelmed by the opulence, the made-up bed, the television set, the chairs, the bathroom, I could tell he had never in all his years passed the night in any place so nice. He walked in, like one of us would walk into some great cathedral, reverently and in a daze. Apple Lisa, who must have seen many motel rooms in her few years, pushed past us, and fell down on the bed and called the Kid over to her. I stayed just long enough to see the Kid pull the pistol out of his pants, lay it on the table beside the bed, undo the button on his jeans and slip them down.

Morales and I went into the room next door. Morales had the telephone in his hands almost at once and was going to call the police, when I took it away from him. "Not now," I said, "we can't turn them over to the law, the way things stand!" Morales was furious, he started saying something to me in that combination of languages he uses when he is excited, but it was so garbled, so run together, that I could not interpret it.

I had no trouble, for instance, that time about three years ago when he ran in to a situation that just flabbergasted him and he was trying to explain it to me. He had been out in a park, some town we were in, a pretty good size town, with a park where hustlers hung out, and he got picked up by some accountant who took him to his house and into the kitchen and then pulled out his balls and laid them on top of a plain pine table and told Morales he would give him twenty dollars if he would give them a good beating with the handle of a ball peen hammer which was there on the drain board by the sink, and the accountant told Morales to be quiet about it because his mother was sleeping, upstairs on the sun porch. Morales had never heard of anything like that, even though he had been in Angola, where I would think that kind of thing would be commonplace, and he was speaking in at least three languages but I had no trouble understanding him, and understanding that poor son of a bitch of an accountant and his sleeping mother, on the sun porch, who was, no doubt, the very cause the accountant had such crazy notions, but here was Morales, as mad as hell because I would not call the law on the White River Kid and sputtering in fury in a combination of languages I could not understand, except, once every twenty words, or so, I could make out *El Niño de Flumen Blanc,* which, as I have already made clear, was his way of saying The White River Kid.

Finally, he gave up trying to convince me and went into our room and took a shower. I followed him inside and also took a shower then I laid down on one of the beds and fell out, I mean, pole axed, and slept like a field hand until three o'clock that afternoon.

I was awakened by Morales, shaking my shoulder. He told me the Kid and Apple Lisa were waiting for me to take them somewhere and get some hamburgers. I got up, washed off my face, got dressed, and went outside to the van. The Kid and Apple Lisa were there, both smiling, and the Kid even gave me a little wave with his hand. I looked to see if he still had the pistol in his belt and sure enough, he did.

It looks to me like a man would be afraid to carry a pistol stuck down in his waistband, especially if they had ever heard about that rock star's bodyguard. It was in Memphis, right outside that place they call the Mid South Coliseum, and it was a cold, rainy night. This ex-wrestler, who was bodyguard for some punk-ass rock star, some pock-faced kid who bit the head off a rat or blew up a live goat on stage, or whatever else they do that passes for music these days, was trying to get something out of the trunk of the limousine they traveled in, and he slipped on some water and the gun he had tucked in his belt, a big caliber automatic I believe it was, fired and the bullet hit him right in the sac and cut through the vas deferens and, for one ball at least, it performed a neat vasectomy. That man was lucky, of course, the bullet doing no more damage than that, but a fellow carrying a pistol tucked in his belt could not count on being that lucky, what he could count on, was having his balls blown to hell, not to mention the bullet probably splitting his thigh bone to pieces.

I could tell the Kid had had a shower. His long hair was soaking wet and had been combed back off his face and was slicked down, "roached over" to one side, as the old folks would put it. He still had on the worn-out blue jeans and jacket he had worn since we had started out. Apple Lisa, too, had taken a shower, and she also had on the same thing. That made me realize, these two had pulled out of Plumrod's Cafe with just what they had on their back and they needed some clothes. I knew I would have to do something about that and I knew exactly what, but first, we had to eat.

5 4

I drove to a McDonald's that was not far away and sent Morales inside for a sack of burgers and fries and Cokes. I hate to eat that sort of thing, but sometimes there is no way around it, and this was one of them.

After they had eaten their fill, and I had had to send Morales back inside for some fried pies, I told the Kid and Apple Lisa that I thought they needed some more clothes and that I was going to take them to where we could get some. What I had in mind was a Salvation Army Thrift Store which I had seen as we drove into town and that is where I headed, stopping first to put more bandages on the Kid's face so the people in the Thrift Store would not recognize the White River Kid and get the notion he had come there to kill them.

The Salvation Army Thrift Store in this town was a pretty big one, better run and laid out than some I had seen. If there is one thing you can say about me, it is that I am an expert, more of a connoisseur of thrift stores, Goodwill Stores, places like that. I have never bought anything anywhere else for years, and traveling like I do, I get to a new one every day. That is what I do for a hobby, visit the thrift stores. You can find something of true value in almost any one. They are all alike, the staff is made up of old men who have been on the bottle for years but who have been off it long enough to be able to make change. Sometimes, they are human wrecks. I was in a thrift store in Panama City, Florida, something with the words Last Chance Mission in its name, and they had three of the worst old alcoholics clerking there I have ever seen, all of them with the shakes so bad they could not get their fingers to stay on the cash register button long enough to open it. You will find alcoholics and drug addicts clerking in Salvation Army Stores, a general line of feebs, mental cases, cripples, midgets, and the like in Goodwill Stores, and society ladies, all young and with some sense of social consciousness, in the Junior League Thrift Store, and I have never found a single item of clothing that was sized correctly. It is something to do with them not teaching much simple math at the exclusive schools where those society ladies get their education, if I am any judge.

The Kid and Apple Lisa were stunned by the things for sale in this particular Salvation Army Thrift Store. They acted like they were in church, like you and I would act if we were turned loose in one of those fancy New York department stores, Bloomingdale's or Lord & Taylor. I was in Bloomingdale's once and walked all over the place and finally came to the place where they sell candy and I saw some chocolates for sale at thirty-two dollars a pound. If I had had the time, I would like to have bought a pound, had them put it in a white paper sack, then gone outside, in front of the store, and stood there on the sidewalk, eating them, while waiting for a bus to take me up-town. As great a piece of fun as that would have been, it would have all amounted to nothing unless there was someone who knew I was doing it, someone to see it, appreciate it, and pass on the facts to some chronicler of offbeat behavior. A prank, or more of a social comment, which is how I would have seen it, eating thirty-two dollars' worth of candy while waiting to take an eighty-five cent bus ride, is lost unless it gets a lot of public-ity, just like Edgar Allan Poe said in "The Cask of Amontillado" that revenge is lost unless the oppressor knows you are avenged.

The White River Kid went right to the rack of blue jeans, he paid no attention to the rack of suits or the rack of sport coats, and I would guess in the environment where he grew up, such items were unknown and had no more meaning to him and would be of less use to him than a deep-sea diver's rubber suit would be to me. The Kid had no idea of sizes, the concept was unknown to him and he asked me what pair to get that would fit him. I got a tape measure from the old reformed drunk behind the counter, and measured the Kid's waist, out of sight of the clerk, I might add, because I did not want him to see me mea-suring that pistol, and then accounting for it by subtracting two inches. When I did, I told the Kid he had a twenty-eight waist. I did not measure the length because I did not know how the Kid might react to my reaching up into his crotch with the end of a tape measure and I told him to hold them up to his waist and see how they looked.

I told the Kid to pick out about three pair of jeans and some shirts and he did, and I picked up a belt about his size and then took him to the rack of used shoes and we found a pair of boots in better shape than those he had and they fit, so we took them, too. Apple Lisa, in her waitress uniform, also picked out some blue jeans and two or three blouses. She had never been turned loose, either, in a store full of clothes and told to buy what she wanted. Both the Kid and Apple Lisa were happy as if they came downstairs from the upper rooms of a great house on Christmas morning and found a lot of gifts under a tree.

Morales, he was not socializing, he stayed in the used book section, looking for pornographic books, even though I have told him time and again that the people who run the Salvation Army Thrift Stores look through all the books donated and cull out the porn. It never gets on the shelves, the staff keeps it, and passes it around in the transients' lodge, so I am told.

I looked for some small antiques while the Kid and Apple Lisa were shopping. I sometimes find pieces of interesting china or little paintings, sometimes big paintings, even, and there are many fine pieces of art on the walls of my house in North Little Rock, Arkansas, where I plan to retire to when I get too old to travel, or whenever I get rich, whichever comes first. I looked at the used record albums. I have a large collection of new, almost unused records that I have picked up in Goodwill and thrift stores, but they are not easy to find. You have to look carefully through all the crap, all the Donny Osmond and Osmond Family and the gospel singers, that get thrown away.

Finally, the Kid and Apple Lisa had lots of clothes and shoes and belts and shirts and blouses, even some used jockey shorts for the Kid. They had too much to carry in a sack, so I picked out a used suitcase for each one and we took it all to the cash register. The clothes were cheap enough, as marked, with the jeans costing two dollars, for instance, but there was some kind of special on that day and the old codger behind the cash register gave us everything for half price.

As he was putting some of the shirts the Kid had bought into the sack, he said to the Kid, "You got a real bargain, here. These shirts is pure-D Oxford cloff!" When he put a pair of the pants the Kid had bought, some type of jean, but with a velvety finish to the fabric, the old man muttered, ". . . hog's down! The finest pants money can buy!"

When we got in the van and started out, the Kid and Apple Lisa started looking through their new clothes, excited, and showing them off to each other. I knew the Kid had never owned so many items of clothing in his life and I called back to him from the seat next to Morales, who was driving, to pick out a package of socks from among the bundles stacked in the back and add them to his clothes.

The Kid's eyes sort of watered out of gratitude and I thought to myself, would he have been any better a boy, would he not have turned out a killer if anyone had ever been kind to him, if he had ever had any sort of security along the way when he was growing up? I answered myself, I guess not, because I knew in my heart the Kid was born a crazy and there was nothing anybody could do about it. He grew up living almost wild along the banks of the White River, and there was never anyone to notice when he acted crazy. The Kid probably started strangling puppies when he was no more than eight or ten. If he had come from a rich family, or even one with modest means but access to the services available, he would have been sent off to some nut doctor, some short little man, screwed up himself, with a lot of wild hair, and a beard with crumbs of dog food in it, and a string of bear claws around his neck, who would have given him lots of tests, using what those nut doctors call "instruments," to find out all humanly possible about him. In the end, the nut doctor would have labeled the Kid some kind of disorder and that would have just about been the end of it. All the nut doctors can do is label mental cases, this one is a schizophrenic, this one is a personality disorder, and so on. If he had come from a rich family the Kid would have been seen by nut doctors all his life, maybe even been hospitalized for periods of time, but in the end he would still be a nut and still end up killing someone, the only difference, the victim's family would know the murder had been committed by a killer who had had all the treatment available.

As soon as we got out of Texarkana, the Kid lay back in one of the bunks and fell asleep, and Morales was back there in the other bunk, also dozing, if not asleep. Apple Lisa came up and sat down beside me in the seat opposite the driver and asked me if the van had a cigar lighter on the dashboard. An odd question, I thought, for I had not seen her smoking but I told her it did and showed her where it was. She opened the purse she had been carrying, and took out a dildo, an artificial penis, a good size one that any man would be proud to have, with a wire coming out the end of it. She pulled out the cigar lighter and pushed a plug on the end of the wire into the empty lighter socket and the dildo started to vibrate. She settled back in the seat, put her feet up on the dashboard, and started rubbing that vibrating dildo against her clit. I have been around, but I have never run into anyone so obsessed with sex as was Apple Lisa. You might wonder how come it was that neither me nor Morales tried to get in on it, how come the both of us were not paying her much attention. Well, first, there was the Kid, a crazy with a gun stuck in his belt, who was traveling with her and who claimed he was going to marry her.

I cannot speak for Morales, but I did not think the Kid would have understood if I had suggested we stop off the road and all of us get it on with Apple Lisa. I have also mentioned earlier that I like to get whipped by a woman, especially an older woman who knows what such behavior is all about, and Apple Lisa did not meet that requirement. Finally, there was the matter of Apple Lisa's looks. She was not a pretty girl, having too much of what the sociologists call "an Arkansas face" to suit me. And she was not a friendly girl, and even spoke sharply to me while she was massaging herself, trying to get off. She had her eyes closed and I would turn to look at her every now and then, and once she opened her eyes and saw me watching her and said, "Quit watching me, you old fart! This ain't none of yours!" and so I dismissed then and there any notion of trying to make it with that ignorant little bitch.

I had more important things to worry about, anyway. Every minute, I was getting in deeper and deeper as far as aiding and abetting the White River Kid was concerned. Not only had I warned him about the deputies waiting to kill him at Plumrod's Cafe, not only had I lied to an officer of the law about seeing him, but I had transported him across a county line and fed him, disguised him, and now, outfitted him with a suitcaseful of clothes. I told myself, and you will remember, I have told you, I got involved at first because I did not want to see the deputies kill the Kid, which is what would surely have happened, since one deputy was lying in ambush outside the cafe door. The rest of my involvement with the Kid, up to this point, had come in slow degrees, and at first was because I was truly afraid the Kid was going to kill me if I did not do as he asked.

But I cannot in all honesty claim that is why I went in deeper and deeper with the Kid. As soon as I realized he was grateful to me for helping him, as soon as I realized he had begun to look on me as a father figure, I was no longer afraid the Kid would kill me. No, I cannot blame the Kid for my getting in deeper and deeper. The truth is, that I myself, Brother Edgar of the Little Brothers of St. Mortimer, and formerly of Romeo, Texas, New Orleans, Louisiana, and now traveling the state of Arkansas as a salesman of factory second and thirds men's socks, am as much an outsider as was ever the White River Kid.

I started out believing everything I was told as a boy, die for your country, behave and you will go to heaven, be honest, and sexual encounters except for procreation are evil and dirty, but I am happy to say I shook off all that and more by the time I was sixteen. I realized that everything is a lie and that, with an exception here and there, people are no damn good. I have lived by this belief and have arrived at the age of fifty-seven as happy as I think it is possible for a human being to be and I have never been troubled by doubts, mental instability, dope addiction, or alcoholism. I do not gamble, I have not brought any children into the world, and I have never undertaken any activities, initiated any movements, which have ever brought one minute's misery on another human being. I have had my disappointments, I have been overlooked here and there, and my talents and perceptions have been ignored when to have listened to me would have provided the world with much blessing. I will give you an example.

I told you I had once written something else but had been disappointed in its reception. It goes back to the days when I lived in New Orleans, shortly after getting out of the army, back when me and Muir Appleblossom were friends and screwing Saraha Stafford in the Dodge Hotel. I had a friend in those days named B Flat Jackson who played the clarinet in one of those clubs on Bourbon Street. B Flat was all I ever knew of his first name. I am sure he had an ordinary first name the same as the rest of us, for I cannot imagine any parent naming their child B Flat, no matter how musically inclined they might be or hope that he would become. B Flat was a bad man for drinking, which is to say, he was drunk all the time and never drew a sober breath. He once went on a real binge with two professors of English at Memphis State University, whom he had met at Tujague's Bar on Decatur Street, and went back to Memphis with them, the three of them tooling along the highway in a Morris Minor, all too drunk to know their own name. Once in Memphis, the two professors ditched B Flat and left him passed out on a street near Crump Stadium in what is called The Garden District. He was out for hours, sort of frozen into a right angle, lying right there on the pavement, where any minute he might have been ridden over by a street sweeper or garbage truck.

He would probably have died, or been killed by someone going through his pockets, had it not been for two old ladies who lived near the corner, who saw him there on the street and sent their yardman down to bring him into their house. These two old ladies enjoyed helping others, were made happy doing good works, and they put B Flat in a bedroom upstairs, bathed him, and tried to feed him. After a day or two, B Flat came halfway back to reality and knew he was in a strange bed in a good house and that two old ladies came and went, tending him.

That first day, he had the notion that there were cats leaping around in the room and jumping up and down off his bed but he dismissed it as the effects of drinking, something he had experienced before, not with cats, so much, as with birds, usually horribly misshapen and carrying dead rodents in their beaks. The cats fought and hissed in his room all day and the old ladies would come in to feed him and not seem to notice the cats so he didn't mention them either, in case they were to get the idea he was crazy or going crazy and call the police to take him away, because B Flat realized he was being well cared for. That night, the cats seemed to get more real, and increase in numbers, and he was able to see them coming and going from his room through an open window. He thought to himself that this must be the worse case of d.t.'s known to medical records and he made another of his periodic pledges to quit drinking.

B Flat passed a fitful night, with the cats fighting each other right there in his bed, and he tried to hide away from his demons by pulling the covers over his head. When morning came, he found three cats in his bed quarreling over the remains of a large, fat rabbit that one had dragged in through the open window and he knew then the cats were real. He tried to count them. There were twenty in his room and when he got up and looked out in the hall there were at least another twenty there and curled up along the stairs. B Flat had never seen so many cats in his life and on top of just having to see them, and dodge their claws, he was beginning to smell them, in fact, the stench of cat feces and urine was almost overpowering.

When the old lady brought in his breakfast, B Flat did not say anything about the cats, just thanked her, and then brushed them away from his tray as they tried to get his food. B Flat decided the old ladies were being held captive by the cats, that there was nothing they could do about them, and he made up his mind to get rid of the cats for them, as a means of repaying their hospitality. He got dressed, felt strong on his feet, and walked around the room, looking for something to use to subdue the cats. He went out in the hall, nobody heard him, the old ladies were all downstairs, with more cats, and he found a croquet set in a closet. He returned to his room and started conking cats with a rock maple croquet mallet. In a few minutes, he had killed outright at least a hundred cats and was getting tired and had sat down to get his strength back, because there appeared to be a steady supply of cats coming up the stairs and in and out his window, when one of the ladies came up with lunch and saw the dead cats and did not like it one bit, saying to B Flat, "But they were our pets!"

The old ladies ordered B Flat Jackson out of their house and swore to each other that they would never again undertake another act of charity. When they called the city to come by and carry away the bodies of over one hundred dead cats, it got in the papers and the city fined the old ladies twenty-five dollars for keeping a cattery without first buying a city license.

When B Flat, who managed to get back to New Orleans, told us about his adventure, it was the first time I had ever heard of the keeping of large numbers of cats, but once I had been made aware of the practice, I started hearing about other people, usually women, with lots of cats in their house. Why would anyone let dozens of cats into their house, to shred the upholstered furniture, cover the floor in feces and urine, and keep one's nerves on end by their lurking and slithering? I did not have the answer until about a year later, when there was a well-publicized death in Nashville, a woman had died at a birthday party and the autopsy said her brain was corroded. It was learned the next day that she lived in a house with two hundred cats, and when the city came out to take them away, the reporters who covered the story noted the overpowering stench of ammonia. Ammonia! Brain corrosion! I was on to something and sat down and wrote a paper, a scientific paper, as it were, just the same sort of thing any scientist does when he discovers something. Why would anyone keep lots of cats when to do so was against all the human instincts for comfort, and tranquility, and sanitation? Addiction, I said.

My thesis was that by keeping cats in large numbers in a home, one becomes addicted to the ammonia produced in their urine, and as in any addiction, the victim needs more and more to maintain a fix. In time, one loses all perspective, ignores the fact that the floor of the house is a sea of fur, that all privacy and comfort disappears, because they are addicted to the ammonia and must have more and more, hence more and more cats. It was as simple as ABC, and I felt I had called society's attention to a danger and that I would be rewarded. I wrote it all out, using examples of behavior suggesting brains damaged by ammonia that I had picked up in my observations and completed a twenty-page paper that should have won me some attention in the world of human behavior. I mailed it to a literary agent, I did not know how to go about placing it in a scientific journal myself, and sat back and waited. In two weeks, I heard from her, her name was Anna Isaac Pitts, and she said she liked it and would submit it to a publisher. In a month, she wrote, saying she had sold it to something called the DuVall Publishing Company, with offices in Dope Haven Springs, Florida. I had never heard of them, but I was not in touch with publishers of scientific tracts, anyway, and left it in the hands of the agent.

My paper was published all right. It appeared in *Hot Beavers of Paris* under the heading Humor. I was paid fifty dollars, of which the agent kept five. I was outraged. My work was important, it should have been published in a scientific journal, I should be ranked along with Junghof and Tarim, the first to observe the correlation between social workers and virginity, and Dalinof, Gumbitzshy, and Sheem, the first to observe the correlation between religion and lunacy; instead, I was thought of as nothing but a humorist. For weeks after that, the agent, Anna Isaac Pitts, kept after me to send her another of my ". . . delightful little send-ups" but I was not interested. My paper was serious, true scientific observation, but it was published in a girlie magazine as humor, along with an article on antique automobiles and some kind of personality quiz to tell a reader if he was a sexual deviate or not. The experience left me embittered, even eager for vengeance against a culture which would tolerate the keeping of house cats in large numbers, not only tolerate it, but often find it quaintly appealing.

Apple Lisa was asleep in the seat opposite me, her mouth hanging open, snoring, with the electric dildo still plugged into the cigar lighter. I unplugged it and let the end of the cord fall down at her feet, which disturbed her a little but not enough for her to return to consciousness. Apple Lisa wasted much of what could have been productive time, sleeping off orgasms.

FIVE

ccording to the map I carried in the van, Block Island was near the place where the borders of Arkansas, Texas, and Louisiana come together. It was not really an island, so I had heard, and I am positive I had heard correct, for there was no water anywhere near there for it to be an island in. As I remember, it was called Block Island because of some factory that was built there in the late 1890s, that made some product called Block Island brand, some kind of fertilizer, maybe, or ice cream freezers, or it might have been ax handles. I remember, in the forties, the place got mentioned in the national news for several days because something there blew up, a big explosion, I cannot remember what caused it but a lot of property was destroyed and about thirty people killed and the newspapers kept referring to it as the Block Island Catastrophe.

That was where we were headed, Block Island, and if I read the map right, it was about forty miles away, dead south. I had no idea what we would do when we got there or how we would be received. I was sure Block Island was a place that had never seen a Brother, like I was supposed to be, where they had no Catholics, which I sometimes tried to give the impression of being, and where the wearing of socks, even in the winter, had not yet caught on. I would be a puzzle to the natives on three or four counts, and that being true, I could expect them to try to rob and kill me, being Americans, even though they were not even in the mainstream.

As I say, I was driving while Apple Lisa, the White River Kid, and Morales Pittman were asleep, Apple Lisa in the seat next to me, and the others on the bunks in the back. I wish one of them had been awake, I wish I had someone to talk to, because the country we were getting into had a strange aspect about it, it looked menacing, grim, bleak, almost devastated. We were on a lonely blacktop road, woods on each side of us, the trees with black trunks, and in places the bark damaged near the ground, where wild hogs had been sharpening their tusks.

Here and there along the road was a house, looking aban-doned, the roof blown half-off, or rotted on its foundation and leaning to one side and once in a while I saw a cow or a horse, always skinny and sick looking. The odor of kerosene hung in the hot air, mile after mile, past dried-up fields and dusty vistas.

When you are in that part of the world, there are no road signs to tell you if you are in Arkansas, Texas, or Louisiana. It was like Apple Lisa had said when I first met her, some say Block Island is in Texas, some say it is in Arkansas. I am sure there are maps in Austin, Texas, and Little Rock, Arkansas, that would tell us for sure where Block Island is located and I am sure neither state is all that anxious to claim it, because I am sure the whole region is nothing but a drain on the state treasury, whichever one it is.

Apple Lisa stirred in her seat and I looked over at her. She was pouring sweat from the heat. She came to and frowned at me and said, "I want a CO-cola." The Kid stirred in the back, and about that time Morales sat up and rubbed his eyes. All three were sweating from the heat because there was no air conditioning in the van and poor ventilation back where the bunks were.

I could have used a cold drink myself and I told them we would stop at the next place we came to, although, I will tell you, if not them, that I had no idea when that would be. I had been on this road one hour and had not seen any inhabited area, no other cars, and nothing to hold out the hope of a place where we could buy a Coke.

As I have said, I never had any children, but I have heard friends who had children tell stories about traveling long distances with two or three children in the car, what trouble it is, what with them always wanting to stop for candy and the like, and I felt a little like that, herding Apple Lisa and her lover the White River Kid along the road to her home. That was another thing, I asked myself, whose idea was it to take the Kid home to meet her parents? I did not think the Kid had any such code of behavior that would make him feel morally and honor bound to ask a girl's father for permission to marry her. It must have been Apple Lisa's idea, yet she impressed me as nothing but an alley cat in heat, and I made a note to try to find out what it was making the Kid and Apple Lisa force me to drive them into this forsaken area.

I had the feeling I was in Transylvania, that at any moment we would be jumped by Dracula and dragged away by him to his castle full of deformed retainers, and sputtering candles, and bats that might really be people. Then I saw a sign on the road that said Socrates, and at once we were in a community and it was just about the most dismal-looking place I had ever seen. Socrates, was it? I saw three or four old brick store buildings, all boarded up, and then, just past them, a gas station and grocery store that was open, and I pulled off the road onto the concrete drive. I looked at the place, sized up the situation, and did not like what I saw. There were three or four of the sort of half-wit old men who sit on benches in front of places like that grocery store, a skinny kid about eighteen, who appeared to be the gas station attendant, and standing next to him were two of the most dangerous-looking men I had ever seen. They were filthy, wearing dirty jeans and walked-over boots caked with cow dung. Both were on this side of thirty, but were

6 8

fat, guts hanging over their belts, and both had dirty black hair, long stringy, and beards that were not really beards, just whiskers that were allowed to grow. One had on a white T-shirt with State Gun Finals printed on it.

I looked at the scene and decided I would not stop, this was not the place to get out and buy a Coke, because I knew we would have trouble. I started the engine and was getting ready to pull out when Apple Lisa pounded me with her fists, and said, "I told you, I want a CO-Cola!" If the Kid had not been there behind me, with that pistol tucked in his belt, and not always on the lookout for wooly gums, I would have busted that little bitch in the mouth and shut her up, but that was not possible, so I turned off the engine, and since Morales was there beside me by now, I said to him kind of on the sly, "I do not like the looks of those two," and nodded toward the men. One of them noticed me and spat out a mouthful of chewing tobacco and wiped his mouth with the back of his right hand. Morales nodded, he agreed with me because he had been around too and knew the scum of the earth when he saw it, but he also understood that we had to stop to keep Apple Lisa from going off in a fit.

I pulled up the emergency brake and opened the door. Apple Lisa jumped out, followed by the Kid, his face still wearing the Band-Aids to hide his butterfly, then Morales and me, and I locked the door. Those two were right there as I got out.

"What you doing in SO-crates?" one of them asked. He pronounced it "SO-crates," to rhyme with "skates," and I knew that somebody years back who had founded this town had come from New Orleans, been run out of New Orleans, was more like it, if the looks of the place and the class of citizen exemplified by these two dirt balls was any indication. They pronounced Socrates "So-CRATES" in New Orleans, mispronounced it, that is, and all the other classic names, too, all the Muses and the Graces, that they have named streets after there.

I looked at the man and answered him, "Traveling ministry,"

I said, and started past him, into the grocery store. I knew by his face that he had no idea what I meant by traveling ministry.

"What's Little Brothers of St. . . ." asked the other one, stumbling over the big word, Mortimer.

"Order of Brothers," I said and I could tell he did not know what I was talking about either.

"What's you got inside there?" the first one demanded. By this time, Morales, Apple Lisa, and the White River Kid were inside the little grocery store.

"Nothing but song books," I said. "Church stuff," and I walked past them into the grocery, where Apple Lisa was pulling on a big bottle of Pepsi and said to me, "Pay this man for our CO-cola!" and she picked up some cookies and candy and threw it on the counter expecting me to pay for that too. I did not want anyone in this vile place to think I had any money, those two outside would kill us for a dime, yet I could not afford to get Apple Lisa upset, so I reached inside my pocket and took out a twenty-dollar bill and handed it to the man behind the counter, just as the skinny kid I presumed to be the gas station attendant came inside and asked me, "Fill 'er up?"

I saw him see the twenty-dollar bill and saw his greedy little face light up, saw his little pig eyes, crossed, too, they were, lit up. I figured the best thing to do was to have that little criminal put gas in the tank and then give him the money, at least, that way, I would have something to show for it. The Kid was drinking a Dr Pepper and not paying any attention to anything, Morales was sipping a Coke, and taking in everything.

"Put in ten dollars' worth," I said. "That's all I got," and he left, heading out to the van. I was glad I did not have the gas tank locked, glad I did not have to give him my keys or he would probably have just got inside and driven it away, he was that crooked looking, and what is more, seemed to be awfully friendly with those two who were hanging around the station.

Two old ladies came in, from out of nowhere, I thought at first, then I realized there were a few unpainted little houses on a street that ran behind the grocery store. They were in flowered dresses, which they had probably made themselves, and they looked like the decent element of the community, if there was one to be found. I bought an Orange Crush and a package of cheese crackers and the man behind the counter added up everything we had bought, rang it up, and gave me the change out of the twenty. I looked through the window outside to where the two men, slouching like night crawlers, were going around the van, looking in through the windows, which I had had the good sense to close before we got out. One of them rubbed the finish of the vehicle and the other kicked the front tire.

"I'm Brother Edgar," I said to the man behind the counter. The old ladies turned up their ears when I said "Brother" and came over to us and introduced themselves, one was a Mrs. Cole, or as she put it "Mizzrizz Cole" and the other was a Miss Calhoun, who said she had been a school teacher there until she retired about three years ago. I have always had a great respect for ladies who teach school in these savage little poverty-stricken villages. They keep the things that mean civilization alive, they put on plays, for instance, something the run of the mill riffraff from these parts would never hear of the whole rest of his life if it had not been for a lonely school teacher trying to bring a little beauty into her world.

"You're in for trouble, Brother Edgar," said the man behind the counter. I looked at him closely. He was bald headed but he seemed clean and his English was good and he talked like an educated man and I quickly realized he was out of place in these surroundings. "You're in big trouble," he repeated and nodded toward the two men, who were now getting into an old pickup truck. I watched as they started the engine and pulled away, slowly, heading south, the direction we were going. "That's the Bunn brothers, J. C. and Houston," the man said, "and they have taken a liking to your van."

I smiled to the man and said, "They are a couple of mean-looking boys, at that."

The man said to me, "They'll make trouble for you. Bad trouble. I know them."

"The Bunn brothers, you say?"

"Houston is the oldest, he's the one with the writing on his shirt. J. C. is the dumb one, dumber than Houston, that is."

"Oh," I said, "I don't expect any trouble out of them. They've even driven away."

"They went up ahead, they're laying for you, up the road a ways," said the man.

The two ladies agreed with the man. "They are evil, Brother Edgar," one said. She put a dime in my hand and asked me to pray that "SO-crates" would be delivered from the Bunn brothers, and then she and the other lady left. The man waved to them and I asked him, "What are you doing here, in a place like this?"

"It's the end of the line," he said. I have noticed that very often total strangers will come up to me and confide things about themselves, things that they ought not to share with every stranger and this man was another, he started in telling me all about himself, how he was stuck here in "SO-crates" because it was the end of the line for him, how he had been ruined by a few morals charges. It came out that he had been a school teacher, too, like Miss Calhoun, only not in Socrates, but some place bigger, more up to date, and how he had not been able to keep a school teacher's job because he could not keep his hands off the boys and how he had lost one job after another when he got caught going down on the whole basketball team, things like that. He was hired to clerk in this little, off-the-road, grocery store and he said that was the end of the line for him and he seemed to accept it.

He said the Bunn brothers knew all about him and razzed him in front of people and picked on him and bullied him, but then, when there was nobody around, they would get him in the back of that store and made him go down on them. I believed him as far as the Bunn brothers was concerned, for I have never known or run across a bully who was not, underneath his tough-guy facade, really a homosexual and the same goes for alcoholics. I could write a really earth-moving scientific paper about the correlation between alcoholism and sexual frustration if I wanted to, for I have never known an alcoholic

7 2

who was not either fighting the urge to make it with one of his own gender or who had had so much poison put into his head by preachers and parents about making it with your own gender that he was just consumed with guilt. Sexual frustration is at the bottom of all alcoholism, but I will not lift a finger to call it to anyone's attention, not after what happened to me when I tried to warn about cat piss ammonia eating away the brain.

I had half a notion to offer to take the grocery clerk out of Socrates, leave as we did, and maybe train him to sell socks, even open up a branch office, set up another traveling van, but I did not, for I had second thoughts about it and will tell you the reason later.

The man went back to warning me about the Bunn brothers and I asked him how mean they were. "They killed a colored man last week, right outside there by that Chevron Regular pump, killed him just for fun, beat him to death with a chain."

"What about the law? Didn't they get arrested? Where's the sheriff, where's the marshal?"

"The sheriff is scared of the Bunns, stays out of their way," said the man. "The Bunns do anything they want, everybody is scared of them, there is no one to bring them to book."

I hated to think of this man, educated, something of a gentleman, stuck here, having to give head to the Bunn brothers any time they took a notion, and all for nothing more serious than pulling a few schoolboys' wieners. "Maybe you can go to a really big city, where a past like you got would not mean anything, and get back into teaching," I said.

"Not a chance. This is it for me," he said. "Yes, my career is over, and to think, all I needed was another three hours to get my master's."

We said good-bye to him, paid the gas station attendant, got in the van, and started out. Apple Lisa fell asleep on one of the bunks as soon as we were on the road, but Morales and the Kid were there beside me as I drove. Morales had picked up all the man was saying about the Bunn brothers laying in wait for us and even the Kid seemed to realize there was some sort of trouble ahead. I could have turned around and gone back the other way but I would have Apple Lisa to deal with when she learned I had traveled away from her family home instead of toward it. So I headed south, along the still-deserted road, traveling slowly through woods that now seemed to be darker and gloomier than I had noticed before.

I turned a curve in the road and saw the Bunn brothers and their old pickup truck, a hundred yards ahead. The truck was parked across the road, blocking it, and the Bunns were standing outside it, waiting for us. I stopped and pointed to the Bunn brothers and said to Morales that there was trouble, trouble for sure. Here I was, on some deserted back road with a wanted criminal in my care, under my protection, you might even say, and there were two country toughs, brains smaller than a sparrow's, who have never worked, never done anything but bullied and robbed and sometimes killed, waiting to fall on me and my van and take anything in it they thought they might use and leave me and the others dead in the road if that was what it would take. If I lived through the next few minutes, there was going to be trouble explaining to the authorities what the White River Kid was doing with us, and us treating him so much like a friend.

I looked in the rearview mirror and tried to see if I could turn around and make a run for it. It did not look like I could, because of the curve and because the road was too narrow, the trees too close to the sides of it, to turn around. That is trouble with a capital T, I repeated to Morales, and it seemed he sort of smiled like he might welcome a little trouble, like he had been too long without any. I tried to get a close look at the eyes of those two Bunn brothers, to see if they looked like the type I could hypnotize, put completely under, and get them to go on their way. You will recall I have mentioned that I worked as a carnival hypnotist for a time and I have hypnotized rubes just like the Bunns time and again, but I will admit the ones I put under probably had more sense than the Bunns, it being my experience that no one, no matter how good, can hypnotize a moron.

I could not see close enough from the distance between us,

so I eased the van up to about twenty yards from them. They both had pig eyes, almost no light in them, making them poor prospects for putting under by hypnotism. I leaned out the window of the van and called to the Bunns, "You fellas move your truck so we can get by." I knew they would not move it, I knew they were eager to jump on us all, rob us, rape Apple Lisa, not that they really wanted to, especially remembering what the ex-school teacher back at Socrates had told us about the Bunns, but it being what men like them are expected to do, it being called for by some code they lived by, and probably try to kill us so they could steal the van. Neither man said a word in answer to my request, both just stood there, grinning in their half-wit, reptilian way, eager to get on with the killing, eager to get to the spoils inside the truck. Houston, the one with State Gun Finals on his shirt, was swinging a three-foot-long piece of heavy chain, probably the very piece he used to beat the colored man to death back in Socrates, a week ago.

"You'all strangers get out of that van!" said J. C., and Houston picked up the idea. "Get out!" he ordered.

I answered them. I said, "Leave us alone, boys. If you don't, you will regret it, for we are under the Lord's protection!" I could tell neither one of the Bunn brothers knew what "regret" meant. My words had no effect on them and I can understand why, for I knew they figured I was just a fat ass old preacher and that Morales and the White River Kid were some kind of holier-than-thou choir boys and that they would have no trouble taking what we had and going off in the van by themselves after they had done with us.

"Get out of there!" yelled J. C.

I turned to Morales and the Kid, both of whom had been watching the Bunn brothers right up front with me, and said, "They got us boxed in, we can't get past that truck, we can't back out. We might as well get out and try to talk to them long enough to see if I can put them under."

Morales knew what I was talking about, he had seen me hypnotize people before and I knew he thought it might work as a way to handle the Bunn brothers. I reached into the glove

7 5

compartment and took out a big gold cross on a long gold chain, an item of costume I sometimes wore when I had to talk to the law in those little towns I sold socks in, and which, I felt right now, I would be lucky to ever see again. I put the cross around my neck and let it hang down, where I could reach it easy and start letting it swing from side to side, to get the Bunn brothers in the mood to be hypnotized. If I could get those two cave men to once set their eyes on that cross, I could put them under, using the old standby line of patter, "You are getting sleepy, sleepy, your eyes are getting tired" and so on. That cross on a chain might work but I would much rather have had a twelve-gauge shotgun in my hand, something I could throw down on them with, something I could use to reason with them, but something I could hurt them with, too, if it came to that.

We got out of the van, me, Morales, and the White River Kid, leaving Apple Lisa asleep in one of the bunks, and stood in front of it, not ten feet from the Bunns, me in the middle, Morales on my left and the Kid on my right. I started swinging the cross back and forth at about the same time Houston drew back with that heavy chain and I knew it was too late for hypnotism.

For some reason, Houston chose to go first for Morales and he took a swipe at Morales's head with that chain for all he was worth and it would have killed him if it had connected, but Morales was not going to die that day. In one easy, graceful motion, he ducked his head and drew that long knife out of his boot and danced right up to Houston Bunn and cut his throat, cut it from ear to ear, as they say, and Houston fell over backwards, his head hanging kind of to one side and blood spurting out of his jugular vein. Morales, seeing he was down, kicked Houston in the balls with his right foot, hard enough for the sound of the impact to echo in the trees. Houston Bunn was out of it and while I know the coroner or medical examiner or whatever they had in those parts would say he died of having his throat cut, from a massive insult to his jugular, if you were to ask me, I would say Houston Bunn died from the same thing that German general said was the most important element in warfare, von Moltke, it was, in some treatise he wrote that was the bible to the German General Staff before World War I, that surprise was the most important element in successful military tactics and if you had seen the expression on Houston Bunn's face as Morales Pittman's knife touched his throat, you would have to say, as I would, that Houston Bunn really died of surprise.

I turned to look at the other brother, J. C. Bunn, and saw that he was on his knees, in front of the White River Kid, who had that pistol out of his belt and pressed against J. C.'s forehead and I saw that the Kid was staring intently at J. C.'s eyes. J. C. Bunn was surprised, too, for this was an unexpected turn of events for him and his brother Houston, who lay there on his back, his neck open like a slaughtered calf's and the rasping of his dying breaths getting softer and softer. This was not the way things were supposed to turn out when the Bunn brothers went skylarking, this had never happened in all their years as the principal bullies in the Socrates vicinity, this was to J. C. Bunn a terrifying turn of events and he looked at me, sweat running down his face, his lip trembling and said, "Who are you all?"

It was a tense moment, I will tell you that, with one man dead, Morales wiping the blood off his knife on the grass, J. C. Bunn on his knees in front of the White River Kid, a man J. C. Bunn might have heard of, if he had never heard of anything else, and I thought I ought to try to ease the tension a little. I thought of telling J. C. Bunn that we were the Little Brothers of St. Mortimer, that we were named after a ventriloquist's dummy, and it even occurred to me in that split second to tell him about Mortimer Snerd, the rube in a straw hat, a rube like J. C. Bunn himself, but with no malice in him and a lot smarter. J. C. Bunn's face contorted into a grimace and he repeated his question, "Who the fuck are you?" I did not get to answer, I did not get to ease the tension, for at that moment, the White River Kid pulled the trigger of his pistol and J. C.

Bunn's head just blew up, went every which way, into a thousand pieces.

The Kid put the pistol back in his belt and returned to the van and I could see him through the window, going back to where Apple Lisa was sleeping, and dropping his pants as he got in the bunk beside her. That left me and Morales and the two Bunn brothers both dead, Houston dying, as I have said, of surprise, and J. C. dying with profanity on his lips. Me and Morales had been in tight spots before, nothing like this one, let me hasten to say, never before were we involved with dead people, but we have had occasion in the past to make quick getaways. Morales went into action first. He ran over to the pickup truck, looked inside, found the keys in the ignition, started it up, and drove it a few hundred yards down the highway to a spot where he could pull it over to one side. Me, I grabbed Houston Bunn's feet and started dragging him into the woods and managed to get him about ten yards off the road by the time Morales returned and we both dragged him a little deeper into the woods. As we were dragging Houston's stinking carcass, I asked Morales if he had been careful to wipe his fingerprints off the steering wheel and the door handle and he said he had, and I asked about the ignition switch, and the key, did he wipe his prints off them, too, and he said yes, and I knew he had, because my experience had shown me Morales Pittman was thorough.

Then Morales and me hurried back to the road and picked up the remains, what was left, of J. C. Bunn and dragged him back into the woods, too. We had both brothers dumped in a spot about twenty yards off the highway and I felt we had done the best we could as far as disposing of the bodies. I do not know if Morales knew about them or not, but I had observed along the way that these woods were filled with wild hogs, Razorback hogs, some call them, I had seen the places where they had gouged the bark off trees sharpening their tusks and from the signs there were plenty of them around, and as far as wild hogs go, there is one certain thing about them, that is, they will eat anything. I have heard of cases where wild hogs have even eaten things like automobile tires, and once, three square feet of fiberglass shingles left on the ground in their path. I had no doubt if the bodies of the Bunn brothers could go undiscovered as long as a full day, there would be nothing left of them, even shoes and clothes would be eaten by the hogs, who easily would rather eat a dead body than tires or shingles.

Morales and me got back to the road and looked around on the ground for anything that might have fallen out of our pockets. I still had my cross around my neck, a lot of good it had done me this time, and I had my billfold, Morales had his. We patted ourselves to be sure nothing had fallen out of our pockets, no pencils, keys, or coins, and once we were satisfied we were leaving behind no evidence that we had been there, we got back in the van, Morales, quiet, in the seat opposite me as I drove and we started out toward Block Island, now about twenty miles away, both shaken, both shocked, but both feeling good about ourselves, too, proud that we had met a danger and overcome it.

SIX

had thought I was in bad trouble back when all I had on
my record, if the police had started to keep one, was
aiding and abetting the escape of a wanted man, harboring a fugitive, and aiding a fugitive in unlawful flight to avoid
prosecution, that fugitive being the White River Kid, who was
passed out alongside Apple Lisa in one of the bunks, both of
them sleeping off another orgasm as I drove the van south to
Block Island, away from the spot where we had had our inter-
lude with the late Houston and J. C. Bunn, but it was no trouble
to what I was in now.

Two men dead and me a party to it, was what it boiled down
to, and that was enough to get me put away in some Arkansas
or Texas prison for fifty years. True enough, they were dead as
a consequence of their own behavior, their ignorance and
greed, in other words, they had brought it on themselves, but
no jury in those parts would see it that way. Even though that
old lady gave me a dime to ask the Lord to deliver Socrates
from the Bunn brothers, and even though they had killed a
colored man with a piece of heavy chain, and even though that

grocery clerk, that ex-schoolteacher, had said they were making his life unpleasant, if it came out that the Bunn brothers were dead as a consequence of meeting us on the open road, we would catch all the fury of the law in those parts. First, we were strangers; that, alone, would convict us of murder. Second, all America loves a bully and while they may say they do not, give them a choice of siding with a local boy who might be said to never do anything more serious than kill a colored man every now and then and beat up a queer whenever he got the chance, or siding with a stranger, a fat old man with a rope full of knots around his middle who travels with a Mexican and another boy whose face is eaten up with cancer, they would go with the bullies every time.

I know you are going to tell me that we killed the Bunn brothers in self-defense and that it was justified. Part of the killing would be justified, I will agree, if we were to get in a real court, where there was an educated man on the bench, and halfway reasonable people on the jury. Part of it? you may ask. Here is how it went, I will explain again, to call your attention to the fine points of the law. The three of us, me, Morales, and the White River Kid, were standing on the road, facing the Bunn brothers, who had deliberately blocked the road with their truck in order to make us stop. We were planning to try to talk to the Bunn brothers, as reasonable men would, to persuade them to let us pass, but before we could so much as say a word, Houston Bunn raised back a chain and made it apparent he intended to injure, if not kill, Morales Pittman, and he had the means at hand to do so, namely, to wit, a length of heavy chain which he had drawn back over his head, and which he actually tried to strike Morales with. So far, we are still in the right, so far we are the innocent parties, faced with sustaining a serious injury, perhaps death, if we do not do something to change things at once, in other words, at this point, Morales Pittman is entitled to defend himself and he did it admirably, actually preventing the assailant from injuring him by killing the assailant, although it is true, he would have to do some explaining about how it was he happened to have a long knife on him at the moment he was put in danger.

At that point Houston Bunn fell back with his throat cut and began to die, we were no longer in any danger from the Bunn brothers, and no longer justified in claiming self-defense for anything else we did. When Morales kicked Houston Bunn in the balls hard enough for it to echo in the trees, he was guilty of an assault on the person of Houston Bunn, not justified by any claim of self-defense, for Houston Bunn was near unto dead and in no position to be able to harm Morales. Still, the kicking of Houston Bunn in the balls and how it was that Morales Pittman happened to have a knife on him are small points that might be explained by the heat of the moment and perhaps the court would take judicial notice of the fact that Morales Pittman was a Mexican and that Mexicans always carry knives, although this is just speculation.

The matter of the death of J. C. Bunn is another thing altogether, for it was plain out-and-out murder, with no claim of self-defense being valid, it being the fact that at the time he was shot by the White River Kid, he represented no threat or danger to us, did not have the means at hand, no weapon, no knife or chain, to pose a threat to us, and was, in fact, disabled by fear and actually on his knees in front of us. It was plain murder, bad enough if the murderer had been an ordinary man and this was his first killing, but the fact was, he was murdered by the White River Kid, a man on the run for already killing six or eight, and a man who went armed for the sole purpose and with the fixed intent of killing people.

So, to sum it up, if the people of Socrates, if that sheriff who was afraid of the Bunn brothers, got wind of the fact that they had been killed by us, they would have been howling after us, and one of the loudest howlers would be that ex-schoolteacher, the grocery clerk, who complained of being abused by the Bunn brothers, howling mad, because we had taken away his boyfriends. That man did not fool me, he could have got out of Socrates anytime a bus came through if he wanted to, but he stayed because he enjoyed being pushed around by the Bunn brothers, he liked it when they pushed him down on his knees, grabbed his ears, made him give them head, enjoyed it for all he was worth, in spite of what he told me. I sort of pitied him, with his playmates gone, the same as I would feel sorry for myself if by some lucky accident, I wound up in a spot with a good-looking woman who understood about my liking to have my ass whipped with a length of fan belt, and who was always there, ready and willing, when I took the notion. That poor man, now he would leave, go to Shreveport or maybe Houston, Texas, and go back into school teaching, and probably wind up a guidance counselor in some public high school, which would be no fun compared to what he had going for himself in Socrates.

Let me say right out in the open, that I do not feel one bit of guilt or remorse for my part in this affair, not even for having transported the Kid from the northern border of Arkansas to the southernmost corner, and put him in a place where he would be tempted to kill another human being, because I did not consider the Bunn brothers to be human beings, and to go back to something I mentioned earlier, I believe society ought to take into account the character, reputation, and past record of criminal or antisocial behavior of the murder victim in fixing punishment for the murderer. I realize this is a novel idea in our society with its silly notion that all men are equal in the eyes of the law, but in truth, I think the Kid ought to be excused for the occasional killing of a man as worthless as the late J. C. Bunn, excused, maybe even honored in some way, perhaps a small pension, or a lifetime pass on the railroads, if we still had any.

My real hope for getting out of this mess lay in two things. First, the hogs. They should eat up every bit of the evidence, if past experience with wild hogs is anything to count on. Even if a part of the bodies were found, the hogs should have done a good enough job to obliterate any evidence of death by bullets or knife blade. Second, that sheriff, the one who was afraid of the Bunns, if I knew human nature, and I consider that to be the one thing I do know best of all, that sheriff would secretly be relieved the Bunns were dead and no longer a menace to his own safety, no longer around to steal and kill in his jurisdiction and make him go through the motions of trying to bring them to justice. And the townspeople, too, if left unvexed, if not forced to act on the information that some of the locals died at the hands of passing strangers, and while still really deep down admiring the bully, would probably be just as happy to let the whole matter die if it could be suggested, if even a reasonable case could be made out, that the Bunns died of misadventure, at the heat of the afternoon, when attacked by a drove of wild hogs.

Attacked by wild hogs? More like, eaten by wild hogs. Imagine if those Bunns had been famous, world figures, important enough to be written up in the reference books, imagine how their entry would read, that is, if it worked out that the hogs got blamed for their deaths, like I was hoping. Imagine an entry in a reference book, Houston and J. C. Bunn, born in Socrates, Texas (or Arkansas), died, Socrates, Texas (or Arkansas), when eaten by wild hogs. Ambrose Bierce, he may have died something like that, his obituary sometimes reads, date of death unknown, but thought to have been eaten by bears. Would you rather be eaten by bears or wild hogs? I cannot say which I would prefer, the bears, maybe, on the theory that it might be quicker, but a drove of wild hogs can polish you off probably just as quick.

It is the notion of death, itself, that distresses me. Dead! To be out of it, to feel no more pain might be desirable, but what about the end death puts to a man's curiosity? That is the bad part of death and I can understand how even a rat, even scum like the Bunns, men who never had a noble thought in their lives, who never listened to a single bird song in their lives, who never did anything praiseworthy, can be angry when death comes, for even a man like that has plans, hopes, ambitions, just like you and me, and while we would surely consider their ambitions disgusting, you can believe they are all important to them and to have them stifled by death is the ultimate insult to a man, be he a Bunn or a Brother Edgar. For death is the end, an end so final we cannot even grasp it and do not even try

8 4

most of the time, but invent stories to help us think it is not really the end after all and lots of people believe those stories and there are many who make big money retelling those stories to those who want to hear them but there are getting to be less and less who believe those stories, the ones about the hereafter and rebirth and heaven and who knows what all else, which is why life in this country is so unsafe, why we all face death every day at the hands of some casual gunman, because practically nobody but wimps and batty old ladies believe you will go to hell anymore if you do not accept your lot here on earth and let yourself be exploited by others. There is certainly no hell to wind up in anymore and as far as punishment here on earth, the only punishment is maybe probation, or at the worst, being sent to prison for life, which means, three years of playing basketball with other prisoners, then release on parole.

The White River Kid stirred in the bunk in back, and got up, pulled up his pants and stood up, brushed his hair out of his face with his hand, and looked down at Apple Lisa, still sleeping. I was getting more and more convinced that that girl had some kind of brain damage, some kind of spells that made her fall into a deep sleep, deeper even than is normal for postcoitus slumber, which you should know by now, she fell into more often than the average girl her age.

The Kid came up front and sat down in the seat opposite me, and said nothing for a long time, just watching me drive, watching the sights along the road. I would guess the Kid could not drive a car and I would guess this was as far away from the banks of the White River as he had ever been. Finally, he touched my shoulder to get my attention and he said, "I want to ask you something."

I knew he wanted advice, it was more of the same thing I had seen developing in him from the first, he was coming to look upon me as a father figure, or if not that exactly, at least an older man, more experienced than him, who could tell him the truth about this and that. When I first noticed it, I was relieved, because it meant less of a chance he might see wooly gums in my eyes and help them escape by putting a bullet in me, but I had lost the fear any sane man ought to have for the White River Kid, and I began to welcome the relationship, I found myself sort of halfway thinking of him as a son, the son I never had, I might add, although I am not complaining and the fact I have no children, nor have ever even been married, is my own doing, a design, you might say, I made for my life, way back, almost before I got drafted, surely by the time I was living in New Orleans, after I got out of the army.

I never wanted children because I had seen the children of friends turn out so bad, so off the mark, that it would have been a heartache I could not have borne to have nurtured a child through his tender years, raised him through boyhood, and then had him turn out bad, become a loan shark, or a free-will Baptist preacher, or a man who never laughed. Here I was, fifty-seven and the nearest thing I would ever have as a son was no rose garden, either, being a boy who probably could not read, and was wanted for killing six or eight, maybe, nine, if you wanted to count that Bunn brother, but I felt good about the Kid thinking of me as a father and I welcomed the chance to pass along all I knew about people and dealing with them to your advantage, because with all the experience I had had in out-of-the-way places, I had picked up more knowledge about human nature than any other man I had ever met. I wish my own father had known half as much about people as I now did, I wish he had given me lots of good advice when I was growing up and maybe I would be something different today, not some near confidence man, traveling through backward villages, trading with country dolts for a living, but maybe a lawyer, even a judge, that being the one job I would like to have, or maybe a clarinet player with a big dance band, but my father had no good advice in him, being a Texas boy, living in the Tri-Cities area all his life and never once doing anything dishonest in his life.

The advice he did give me was almost all foolish, pure silliness, most of the time, such things as I was always to keep women on a pedestal, and nonsense such as that. The only advice he ever gave me that was at all, even remotely sound, was never to buy a new hat on the same day I had a haircut, but with the wearing of hats a thing of the past, and haircuts, too, almost a thing of the past, that advice is not even valuable anymore. I had a friend in the army, a man named Juggins, from Minnesota, who was interested in wild animals, particularly monkeys and who later became a zoo director and was founder of the St. Paul Primate Festival, who told me the only advice he ever got from his father was never to force a wet fart. He married a soprano named Marianna Quicksilver who had once lived with the Russian diction coach at the Metropolitan Opera Company, and while Juggins has nothing to do with this story, I mention him only to let you know that I have had what some would call high class friends in my time, and I have not always palled around with ex-convicts, killers, and ignorant farmers who rarely wear socks.

So I smiled at the Kid and said what is it? He was silent a minute, like it was taking him time to get up his courage, or like he was just not used to talking to people, then he nodded his head over his shoulder in the direction of Apple Lisa, and said, "She's taking me home to meet her people," and then he said nothing and I said nothing, either, I figured it best to just let him tell me what it was he wanted to tell me. After a while, he said, "What am I supposed to say to them?"

I tell you, that warmed my heart, that question. Here he was, really asking for my advice on a matter of great importance to him and that made me feel more useful, more important, than anything that had happened to me in a long time.

It also answered a question I had posed earlier, about whose idea it was for the Kid to come all the way from northern Arkansas to southern Arkansas to meet a family of what would surely be riffraff, scarcely likely to care who one of its offspring married, just hopeful it was someone with some money, any money, no matter how ill-gained. I knew the Kid needed a father's response and I tried to think of exactly the right one, but in order to do it, I was going to have to have more information from him, so I started gently, very gently, for he still had that pistol stuck in his belt, asking him questions.

"You say you just met Apple Lisa, back yonder in Como, about the same time I first laid eyes on you?"

He nodded in agreement, and said, "I ain't never set eyes on her before I went in that cafe and when she set down that hot dog she said let's you and me fuck. That's the first time I ever had a word out of her."

"When did you decide to get married?" I asked.

"When we was hid in the back, yonder, under all them socks."

I wanted to play the father role completely, so I asked the Kid if he really wanted to get married and he said, he guessed he had to, now. Apple Lisa was counting on it and was taking him home to show off to her mother and father. Yes, he said, he guessed he wanted to get married since it was so important to Apple Lisa and anyway, as he put it, "it weren't no big thing, either way."

I asked him where they planned to live and he said, her hometown, where we were headed, which he called Black Island, instead of Block Island, and when I asked what he would do for a living, he said Apple Lisa told him he could go to work for her father. I asked the Kid what her father did and he said he did not know.

There was one thing I wanted to know and I felt it safe to ask the Kid and I did. "Does Apple Lisa know who you are? Does she know why those deputies were looking for you?" and he said, "Who I am? I don't even know who I am." And I let the rest of the question drop and just thought it a safe assumption to guess Apple Lisa did not know all that much about her intended, but I did want to follow up on the Kid's statement that he did not know who he was, and I asked, "What is your name?" and he just shook his head from side to side and said, "All I've ever been called is the Kid, but I think my full real name is White River Kid." I almost broke out crying, to find a human being so much let alone to raise himself that he did not even know his own name, but I did not cry because I was trying to act like that boy's father should have acted and fathers do not cry without more reason than I had.

"You are going to have to have a real name when we get to Block Island," I said, "something folks can call you, something Apple Lisa can call you when she introduces you to people."

The Kid smiled. "Apple Lisa! That ain't no real name, is it? Names is something, ain't they."

I told the Kid it might be easier if we told everyone his name was W. R. Kid, no names, just initials, that way, it would not be hard to remember, or so I thought. He had never heard of W and R and I tried to explain they were letters of the alphabet, but he did not know what alphabet was, either. I asked him if there was any name he would like to have, was there anything he would like to be called if he had his way, and his face lit up, the brightest face I have ever seen and he said, "Bird!" "Bird?" I asked, and he nodded and he made his right hand into a bird, thumb and little finger for wings, the other three for the body, and started moving it gracefully around over his head, like a bird in flight. "You know about birds?" he asked. I said yes. He said if there was one thing he would like to be it was a bird, just about any bird, except the kind of big rough birds that eat dead things along the river. "Bird" seemed workable enough to me and so the Kid and me agreed we would tell Apple Lisa and her family, and Morales Pittman, too, that he was Bird. "Bird" would be enough name for the folks in Block Island, if I was any judge of things, but there was a more important matter to take up with the Kid and that was the matter of the butterfly tattooed on his face, a dead giveaway it was, to any law enforcement officer, for there were not that many young white men with long stringy hair and butterflies tattooed on the left cheek going around at any given moment. Sooner or later, probably sooner, some law officer, maybe even some half-drunk town marshal would spot him and lay for him somewhere and kill him outright, from ambush, for the papers had made the Kid out to be more than I thought he was in the way of being quick as a rattler, and always on the prowl, and no ordinary peace officer along the road we were traveling would have the courage to try to arrest him peacefully, but would try first to kill him before the Kid could throw down on them.

Morales Pittman woke up and came up to the front and stood behind us, yawning and looking relaxed, in spite of having not an hour earlier killed a man with a knife. Morales might take to killing with no qualms and we knew the White River Kid did, but I do not mind telling you, it will be a long time before I forgot the sight of Houston Bunn with his throat gaping open and J. C. Bunn with his head completely missing. It not only would be a long time, it would probably be never. I felt that I would live out my life and die of old age without ever getting over the shock of that horrible sight, and this may surprise you, for without intending to, I may have given you the impression I have spent a lifetime wading through blood and guts, but that is not true. Before today, before being in on the Bunn brothers getting their just deserts, the only blood I had ever seen was while in the army when I once came up on a man who had just had his leg cut off by an airplane propeller. He had been trying to prop it, the airplane that is, by pulling the propeller down to turn over the engine, and he had his right leg up and the thigh parallel to the ground when that engine caught hold and fired up and the propeller came chopping down on his leg, cutting it off in mid-thigh. There was a crowd there, some of his fellow airplane mechanics and two or three officers, two of those young second lieutenants I was, unknown to the higher-up, writing evaluations of, and an old captain, who had been a combat infantryman in Italy in World War II, but who was now a lonely old drunk, who was considered unreliable and not thought much of by the rest of the officers.

Well, the sight of that blood and cut off leg was too much for those two young second lieutenants, both of whom, I recall, had been cheerleaders in college, and one started vomiting and the other just stood there, clutching his balls. But the old captain had seen blood and stubby leg ends before and, just like the old fire engine horse reacts when he hears the fire alarm, he automatically started tending the man, putting a tourniquet around his leg, barking out to call the helicopter, putting his jacket on the man to keep him warm, to keep him from going into shock. The man was raised up on his elbows, with no unusual look upon his face, his leg, with his boot on the foot, laying a distance away. If that old captain had not been there, that man might have died, but that captain did what officers are supposed to do, he led, and that man can be thankful he was there and that the matter was not left in the hands of one of those cheerleading second lieutenants or he would have died, although this is not to rule out that one of the enlisted men, standing around, even me perhaps, might have jumped in and acted like an officer, might have done the same thing as the old captain did, might have risen to the task as it came up, for as Napoleon said, there is a field marshal's baton in every soldier's knapsack, which I have always considered to be one of the most profound utterances ever attributed to anyone.

As I said, Morales was in good spirits. Probably knifing someone brought back the good old days when he was in prison, a lot younger and better looking, and getting butt fucked six or eight times every time he took a shower, and he put his arm around the Kid's shoulder and made some jovial remark to him, which the Kid did not understand because of Morales's language problem, but which I understood to be something along the line of, "We showed those two, didn't we, *El Niño de Flumen Blanc!*" Then Morales said to me, "Yeah, I was careful to wipe off the steering wheel and the door handle on that truck real good." The Kid understood enough of that statement to be puzzled and asked me why Morales had wiped off the steering wheel and door handle of the truck and I said, "Fingerprints," and the Kid repeated the word, "Fingerprints," and I knew he had no idea what I was talking about. I started to explain, about how oils in the human fingers leave distinctive prints on objects they touch and I knew it was all news to him and so I asked him if he had ever been fingerprinted, and I explained what was involved, pressing your fingers against an ink pad then on a piece of clean paper and the Kid shook his head and said no. *No?* Could I believe that the Kid had never been fingerprinted in his life?

I did believe it but I questioned him further, such as have you ever been arrested? No. Have you ever had handcuffs on, have your hands ever been chained together? No. Have you ever been in jail? No. I was convinced that the Kid, or Bird, as I now wanted to start calling him, had never been in custody and that it was almost a certainty that there were no fingerprints of him on record. Photographs? What about photographs, I asked him. Has anyone ever taken your picture? No.

Inside myself, where a man tells himself the truth, the honest to goodness truth about himself and about others, the truths he never says in public, I knew that there was no hope for the White River Kid. He was born crazy and there was no chance for him, he would die from a peace officer's gun somewhere on up the road, maybe in a week, maybe in a year, but it was certain, there was no hope of rehabilitation for him and no way to close our eyes to the fact that he was a serial killer and all the glories of western civilization demanded he be brought to justice, justice in the Kid's case being locked up for life in a mental hospital, if he did not get killed first.

I had some crazy notion, born slowly since it was first apparent the kid looked up to me, of trying to get him set up away from his White River, somewhere where he might feel safer and maybe never kill another human being. Living away from almost all the rest of the world in Block Island, working for Apple Lisa's father, might be what would work out for him, but first, I had to do something about that tattoo and I spoke out, with no ifs, ands, or buts, directly to the Kid as he sat next to me.

"Kid . . . er Bird . . . that is, you don't have a chance in hell with that tattoo on your face." The Kid reached up and touched the spot, which was still bandaged, still covered by a Band-Aid, that place and the others I had covered to throw off the curious. "That butterfly on your face is just like a sign that says I AM *the White River Kid, come and get me!* and any deputy that sees it is going to start shooting at you first and ask questions later. It has got to come off!"

The Kid looked puzzled. "It won't come off," he said. "It's on there for good, it won't even come off with coal oil!"

I know you are asking me what I could do to get a tattoo off the face of the White River Kid, tattoos being permanent as everybody knows, as every man who ever got drunk and had some disgusting representation tattooed on his arm will tell you. I had a friend in the army who had a large heart and flowers and the word *Mom* tattooed on his arm and he hated it, he felt like a fool with some statement of I Love Mom on his arm and as he put it, "I have to stay off the beach. I can never go to some nice resort in the summertime." It is true that tattooes are permanent, but they can be removed and when I was telling the Kid his tattoo had to be removed for his own safety, I had in mind the ministrations of my old friend Doc Poole of Hot Springs, Arkansas, who had removed tattoos in the past from the bodies of other men wanted by the law, chief among them the late Sweet Eddie Yates, Bennie the Blind Fruit, and Clovis of Clovis, New Mexico, all of whom were New York City types, and probably richly deserving of being put behind bars, but who escaped that end, thanks to Doc Poole, long enough to die at the hands of other New York types, which is the one redeeming feature of the big-city criminal element.

"That tattoo has got to come off, Kid, and I have a friend who will do it and it won't hurt a bit. Once it's off, gone without a trace, you can go around town without that bandage and no one will know who you are and you'll be safe."

The Kid shook his head. "I don't want to get rid of it. *No!*" I knew the Kid was naive, not wise about life, but I did not foresee any problems in trying to get him to get rid of his tattoo if it meant a chance to go on living, and I asked him, why not. Why was it so important? The Kid said, "It brings me good luck!"

Good luck? I could not believe my ears! What good luck had the White River Kid ever had? His mother was not able to take care of him, he got put in foster homes, got whipped, ran away, got brought back, got whipped some more, finally ran away for good and lived by his wits, eating raw fish, stealing, fucking sheep, going crazy and thinking he saw wooly gums here and there, killing people, on the run, what good luck could he ever have had, and I asked him, I said Kid, I don't understand why

9 3

you think that butterfly is good luck, what good luck have you ever had with that thing on your face? and the Kid answered right back, "I met you!" and he smiled. I mean to tell you, I almost broke out crying, to think that there was someone, even a hunted killer, who was glad he had met me, for to tell you the truth, I do not have that many friends, have never really been what you could call popular and sometimes feel that people I meet consider me a pest, especially whore ladies whom I try to get to slap my bare ass with a fan belt, but I did not cry, instead, I cleared my throat and said to Apple Lisa, who was now standing behind me, "Young lady, I don't think you know this boy's name, do you?" and of course, she did not know his name. It had been my observation that there were probably times when she did not know her own name, and she surely did not know her fiancé was the notorious White River Kid because Morales and me had never mentioned his identity in her presence. Apple Lisa frowned at me and asked, "What are you calling me a young lady for?" but I ignored her question and pointed to the Kid and said, "His name is Bird!" and she looked at me and I could see the wheels trying to turn over inside her brain and finally she asked, "You mean like a flying bird?" and I said yes and she turned to the Kid and asked him "What kind of a name is that? Is that all the name you got?" and the Kid nodded and that was the end of that.

We were on the outskirts of Block Island and Apple Lisa started getting excited as she saw familiar places. I asked her how long she had been away from home and she said she did not know exactly, maybe a long time, maybe not so long. Apple Lisa was clearly one of those people who cannot tell big from little. I had no idea what was going to happen when we got to her parents' home, or how Morales and me would be accepted. At first, I thought as soon as we got to Block Island, I would try to shake Apple Lisa and the Kid and get back to my business of selling socks but along the way down to Block Island from Como, I had changed my feelings about the Kid and was now actually feeling good about him. I had hopes of his reformation and thought that all it might take was a little security, and part of that security was getting that tattoo removed from his face, a task that would be ten minutes work for my friend Doc Poole in Hot Springs. I had planted the idea in the Kid's brain of letting me take him to the doctor and get it removed, and he was not keen on it, but I hoped he would agree after thinking it over for a day or so, and to get him to want to do it, I planned to keep lots of bandages on his face.

SEVEN

We arrived in Block Island, Arkansas, or, maybe, Texas, or perhaps, Louisiana, late in the afternoon, at its north end, where the factory that blew up in the forties had been and where both sides of the road were lined with abandoned machinery, acres of it, strange-looking equipment the likes of which I had never seen before, three-sided storage tanks, for instance, and odd-looking gears, bigger than anything I had ever run across, and pipes and wide metal bars and flat plates with circular holes in the middle of them, and old truck bodies and drag lines and scaffolds and hoists, all rusted up and nearly covered with kudzu, of no interest to anyone for nearly fifty years and now not even worth hauling away for scrap.

Just past all this castoff, on the left side of the road, and about fifty yards back from it, was the biggest hole in the ground I had ever seen, not counting things made by nature, like Mammoth Cave and the Grand Canyon, but man-made things, like this hole, which must have been created when the factory exploded, and I mean to tell you it must have been some explosion because that hole was about five hundred yards deep in the middle.

Me and Morales and the Kid looked at all that metal and that hole with something like reverence, me for sure, and maybe Morales, too, thinking about how many must have died and how much it upset so many people's lives. I would guess the Kid did not know what to make of it, and had no idea what caused it, or even that it was caused since he had seen so little in his time, and Apple Lisa, who, of course, had grown up on the brim of that hole, paid it no attention, but was giggling and squirming at other things she saw that told her she was home.

That reminded me I intended to ask her someday if I got to where I thought I knew her well enough, how come it was that she was waiting table nearly three hundred miles north of here when we first ran on to her and why it was she had ever left Block Island in the first place.

Block Island was the creepiest looking, most backward community I had ever seen, and to get out of it to go anywhere would be an improvement, but as far as Apple Lisa and why she left Block Island, I could not guess, for I did not read her as having enough sense to realize Block Island was the end of the universe. If I had to guess how she got out, it would be that she got taken up by someone passing through who met her by accident, found her a good screw, and took her along with him to wherever he was going and later got rid of her or lost her.

Block Island had one street, most of the buildings along it boarded up and long abandoned, but there were about a hundred yards of Main Street with business along it, a beer joint called Bud's, a grocery store, a cafe, a couple of other buildings with something to do with auto parts in one and more beer in the other.

Apple Lisa directed me along the street, pointing to a side street about a block ahead, telling me to turn right there, and I did. It was called Dunrad Street and it was plain dirt with old motor oil poured on it by the highway department to keep the dust down. I noticed the other streets off Main were all dirt with oil poured on them and the heat and the oil smell brought back the sensation of being ten years old again in Romeo, Texas, on hot afternoons, when they had just poured fresh oil on the dusty road to settle it down, how there was no way to get anywhere in town without getting old motor oil on your shoes and how after a while, maybe two weeks, that oil would seem to settle into the ground and then would not come off on your shoes and how after years of having oil poured on it every summer, sometimes two or three times a summer, the street would take on sort of a paved or blacktopped appearance and the dirt road would at least become well defined.

Apple Lisa directed me along Dunrad Street for about thirty yards to the intersection of another dirt road called Clapp Street. That was where she lived, at the intersection of Dunrad and Clapp, and she pointed to a house where an old man was sitting on the porch, a barefooted old man in bib overalls and a straw hat, sitting on the porch above a lawn littered with weatherbeaten rabbit hutches and old minnow buckets and said to stop there, which I did. I opened the door and Apple Lisa got out and waved to the old man and yelled, "Daddy!" and the old man sort of came out of a reverie and looked at her close and said, "Liser? Is that you, Liser?" and Apple Lisa ran up on the porch and hugged his neck and the old man hugged her back and took off his hat and sort of rubbed his eyes with the sleeve of his shirt, then he called over his shoulder to someone in the house to come outside and see who was here. By this time, me and Morales and the Kid were outside of the van, standing there in front of the house. I noticed the Kid still had that pistol stuck in his belt and I motioned for him to get back in the van and I told him if I was going to meet my father-in-law for the first time, I would not have a pistol stuck in my belt because it might give him the idea that I was not the man his daughter should marry. If it was me, I would put my pistol in my suitcase before I went up to meet the old man for the first time and the Kid listened to me, and somewhere in his brain the notion made sense and he took out the pistol and did put it in his suitcase, then caught up in the rituals of meeting fathers-in-law for the first time, he ran his hand through his long blond hair and sort of put it in order, then he and I got out of the van again.

By this time, three people had come out of the house, a young man about twenty, with some of his lower teeth missing, who looked like Apple Lisa and who I assumed must be her brother; a boy about eleven, sickly, eyes draining some sort of phlegm, no chin, skinny, bad teeth, head sort of hanging to one side; and then something I will just call a creature, for that is what it looked like at first, some sort of creature, its sex not discernible at first, but weighing about seventy pounds and as old at least as the old man on the porch. I was sure it was wearing a wig, the darkest of jet black, and jet black sideburns painted on its face, sideburns that came down to the edge of the jaw and then flowed out into mutton chops. This thing was wearing some sort of Halloween costume, some kind of a heavy tunic and tight pants, both made of some kind of fabric that probably glowed in the dark, and black vinyl boots, and it had a white scarf tied in a knot around its neck.

Apple Lisa saw this human being, in the strange get up and cried out to it, "Mommer! You sure do look good in them new clothes!" Good, was it! To me, the creature, whom I now accepted as being Apple Lisa's mother, looked like a Paiute medicine man, done up in his work clothes to try and drive out an epidemic of smallpox that was killing off the tribe. But a spectacle or not, she hugged Apple Lisa and said, "Liser, baby, he done cured my cancer!"

"Who done cured your cancer, Mommer?"

"E'vis done it!" E'vis?" "E'vis Presley! He done cured my cancer! I prayed to him and he looked down and saw me suffering so and he must have just waved his hand or something and told the cancer that was eating me up to go away, and Liser, baby, it started to go away and that was when I got the notion that if I was to dress up and look just like E'vis, and sing his songs out loud, it would leave out altogether, and that's what I done, and that's what it done!"

"Mommer, you mean you ain't got no more cancer?" asked Apple Lisa, and the old lady, her mother, said "Nairy a bit!"

then she looked at me and said, "I had me a cancer the doctor said was as big as a Twinkie," and the old man, Apple Lisa's father, spoke up and said it was true that "mommer" did not have any more cancer and they had "E'vis" to thank for it.

I think I should pause here in this story and explain to those who might one day read it, just who Elvis Presley was and why it came to be that this cancer-stricken old woman had the idea Elvis had relieved her of it. Elvis Presley was a singer and movie actor who lived in his idea of splendor in Memphis, Tennessee, until 1977 when he died from taking too many drugs. He was a kind of magnet, only instead of attracting iron filings, he drew nuts, mostly women, but lots of men, too, all lonely misfits, but drawn to him and his tawdry lifestyle in such large numbers as to be totally inexplicable, except perhaps the batty females thought of him as the son they never had, "a boy who was good to his mother," as if most people are not good to their mothers, as if being good to one's mother was so rare that the occasional man who was deserved to be idolized for it.

"Where did you get this idea of praying to Elvis?" I asked the old woman. I concluded at once that she was insane, but she did not look dangerous, only ludicrous and I thought I would have a little fun with her, even goading her, if it came to that, for I have always been repelled by Elvis's persona and particularly by his followers who see in his sordid life some sort of glitter which they find enviable.

"Brother Tonic told me to pray to him," she said.

"Brother Tonic?" I asked, thinking for a moment there was another act like mine on the road in that area, one that might have played there, which is to say, might have been there selling socks like I do, in the not too distant past. Brother Tonic, it turned out, was a man named Ricky Tonic, who was pastor of some snake-chunking tabernacle about three miles away, who did Elvis impressions in the pulpit, and who held that Elvis was not dead, only hiding out "till it all blows over!" only what it was that had to blow over was not brought out in his sermons. Apple Lisa's mother did not accept her pastor's theory that Elvis was still alive. "He's dead, as far as earthly goes," she said to me, "and he ain't yet been received into the Kindon of Heaven. For the next three thousand and sixty-one years, all he's going to have to do is fly around up in the sky, looking down on the earth, and helping people in trouble, when he hears them praying to him, and singing his songs and dancing to them," she said. I took up the idea of "flying around" and asked her exactly how he did it and she said she had seen him, that he was sitting in the middle of "a great ole big" airplane wing, just a wing, no cabin, no cockpit, nothing but just a wing, flying around aimlessly in the sky, "about six miles up," Elvis sitting in the middle in a straight-backed chair.

"Is he alone on that wing?" I asked.

"No! They's cats on it with him!"

"Cats?" I asked.

"Cats! Maybe as many as six or eight hundred, all of them just sitting there on the wing with him, waiting to serve him."

What could a cat do for Elvis Presley that he could not do for himself, I asked myself, but I did not ask her, for I realized a gentleman, even one who was always disgusted by Elvis fanatics, would not pursue the matter with an old woman as out of it as this one was.

After the old woman finished talking about Elvis, there was silence, nobody said anything and we all were just standing there, no one knowing exactly what to do, or what was expected. Apple Lisa had not introduced us or given any explanation to her parents as to who we were or why we were there or how she came to be in our company. The White River Kid was fidgeting, I presume because he thought he should, right then and there, ask the old man for his permission to marry Apple Lisa, who had sat down in a swing at one end of the porch and who was swinging back and forth, as fast as she could and as high as she could, almost touching the ceiling of the front porch. The one who looked like Apple Lisa's brother, the one who was about twenty, could not take his eyes off Morales Pittman. The old man, Apple Lisa's father, had sort of withdrawn from the scene, and was just staring off across the field in front of the house. The old woman picked up a broom and started sweeping the porch and after a while, she said, over her shoulder, to me, "You all stay for supper?" and I answered that we would like to. Apple Lisa got out of the swing at the mention of supper and asked her mother what she was fixing and the old woman said rice and gravy and a little salt meat, which must have been Apple Lisa's favorite food because she jumped off the porch, turned a handspring in the grass in front of the house, and ran off down the road, yelling, "Oh boy! Oh boy!" That left us all once again, with nothing to say, all just looking at each other, except for the old man, who did not seem to even be aware we were there.

I could not wait for Apple Lisa's family to introduce themselves and I put out my hand to the old man and said, "I'm Brother Edgar!" The old man smiled, much the same way as the White River Kid had, when I first met him, and it was obvious to me that I must have been the first person ever to want to meet him, and I immediately felt good toward the old man, I knew he was all right, and he kept on smiling and holding on to my hand. "I'm Baker Weed," he said.

So, this was the Weed family, was it, that meant Apple Lisa was Miss Apple Lisa Weed, which was a name she was going to have to drag herself up past, if she ever hoped to amount to anything, although I had observed that she was not too bright and would be lucky, the White River Kid aside for a moment, to marry some man in the neighborhood who made a living stocking ponds. The old woman said "I'm Mizzrizz Weed." Mizzrizz, that is a way you hear Mrs. pronounced in some parts of Arkansas and Tennessee and probably elsewhere in the south, and while it does not mark a person as an idiot to say Mizzrizz, it does mean he would not be able to tell you who Sibelius was or what Wyoming is. Baker Weed introduced the rest of the family, Apple Lisa's oldest brother, the one without any front teeth, was Reggie and the eleven-year-old boy, with the draining eyes and no chin and a host of visible neuroses, was her younger brother, named Elvis Weed. I could see that Reggie and Apple Lisa had the same father, but it was not so certain that their father was also Elvis's father, but I did not spend any time pondering the matter.

I introduced Morales as my assistant and then I introduced the White River Kid, whom I had earlier decided to call Bird, as "W. R. Bird, no name, just initials," since it seemed like it would work better, both for Morales and me and for Apple Lisa's family, the theory being that an assumed name as near to your own name, especially if you can keep the same initials, just comes easier, is less trouble to remember when things get busy.

When I had finished introducing us, Apple Lisa's mother asked me if I was a preacher, since I called myself Brother and I tried to tell her a little something about the Little Brothers of St. Mortimer, without going into details and I told her we did "good works." Then she asked where we had met "Liser" and she said she and her husband had assumed she was dead, since she had "run off" about a year ago and they had not heard from her and no one had laid eyes on her in all that time. I explained that we had met her up in Como, Arkansas, where she was "working" and then I saw a chance to make it easier for the Kid and I told Apple Lisa's parents we had driven her and "Mr. Bird" down here to Block Island to meet them because Apple Lisa and him were engaged to be married. The old man smiled but Apple Lisa's mother was not all that excited about the idea and asked the Kid what he did for a living. Before the Kid could say anything, I spoke up for him and said Apple Lisa had said he could go to work for her father in his business. Apple Lisa's mother laughed and pointed to the old minnow buckets and the old rabbit hutches in the front yard and said, "That's his business!" Then she called across the porch to the old man and asked, "When was the last time you sold one?" and he, still, looking off, said, "It ain't been that long." And she came right back and said, "He ain't sold nothing in all the years he's had them buckets and rabbit boxes out there. Back when he got out of the army, he took his saved-up army money and bought them buckets and some fishing poles and built them rabbit boxes and thought he was going to get rich, selling them. He ain't sold a one and that's been since 1954! If he didn't have his army pension, we'd a starved out years ago!"

I had seen the brand-new car in the yard and thought the family must have some money and I looked at the car again and the old man saw me and must have read my mind and he said, "That's Reggie's car. It ain't none of ours. Reggie bought it when he got ten thousand dollars for getting his teeth knocked out in that accident."

Baker Weed explained that Reggie had been walking down the highway and a truck owned by Little Rock Aluminum Nipple Company had passed him, turned a corner, and a piece of pipe on the truck had struck Reggie in the mouth, knocking out his front teeth. He had got a settlement, the biggest and easiest money anyone in the family had ever seen and he went out and bought a car, and spent it all, and did not save anything to get his teeth replaced, but that was no problem because he already had two other lawsuits for personal injuries pending, one against the Kroger Store in Little Rock, for allowing him to slip on something ". . . ice cream, I guess . . ." near the Courtesy Booth, resulting in a damaged spine and constant headaches, and another against a department store in Texarkana, Texas, for allowing "an ammoniated substance" to seep through the walls of the second floor men's room, which caused Reggie permanant lung damage when he went into the rest room to wash a sample of Mrs. Munsey's Chocolate Croissant off his hands and unsuspectingly breathed the fumes. Lawyer Clifton Bearclaws, of Little Rock, was suing the two companies for Reggie, on contingency, and had assured him he would recover substantial damages in both suits, leaving Reggie, after Lawyer Bearclaws's percentage was deducted, with more than enough to get him some false teeth in the front and plenty left to do something for his old parents.

Reggie's parents appeared to approve of his activities, indeed seemed pleased that he had found a way to make a living that left him so much free time. I had seen Reggie's type before, he was nothing but a low schemer who starts out trying to live on the proceeds of damage suits and finally comes to believe he really is disabled and applies for his social security or disability grant because he thinks he is unable to work and who gets rejected the first few times he tries, but has enough tenacity to hang on and keep reapplying until finally his application is approved. Reggie now had a big new car with a vinyl top and factory air but unless someone gave him ten dollars, unless he got some money quickly, he would not be able to keep gasoline in that new car on the lawn, which by its presence there, mocked the Weed family, in their slat-board house with their supper of white rice and salt meat on the table.

Apple Lisa's father, whom I have been calling Old Man Weed, but who was really a few years younger than I am, asked "Mizzrizz Weed" how soon until supper. She said she had not put it on yet and he told her to get in the kitchen and get it ready. She quit sweeping, muttering something about ". . . too many chiefs and not enough een-yuns!" and went into the house. Elvis Weed spoke up, the first thing he had said since we had been there. He asked the Kid what were those bandages all over his face. I decided to let the Kid handle this one himself, without answering for him, but I did catch his eye and nod to him and smile and let him know he should answer because I felt the White River Kid would not feel intimidated talking to the likes of Elvis Weed, an eleven-year-old kid, who looked very troubled, and I was right, because the White River Kid answered him without any hesitation, and said, "My face is eat up with something!" Reggie said maybe his mother would pray to E'vis to ask him to cure it, since it would be no trouble, since the Kid was going to be family. I asked Reggie why his mother did not pray to "E'vis" to cure his ammonia-damaged lungs and his out-of-whack spine. Reggie looked sheepish and said, sort of twisting himself into the ground, that he did not really have lung and spine trouble, that he was just claiming he did to be able to have enough money to get some false teeth in the front of his mouth. He said he had heard a place advertise on television, late at night, that they could fix up false teeth for anyone, no matter how messed up their jaw was, by just talking to them over the telephone and all it cost was twenty-six

1 0 5

ninety-five, cash or credit card. False teeth fitted over the telephone, that is an idea I had never had, I am sorry to say, since I might have made a lot of money out of it, although I probably would not have undertaken to do it, if I had thought of it myself years ago, on the grounds that even in America there were not enough fools to make it a paying proposition. But here I was, standing in the presence of a typical American boy who bought the idea all the way down the line and who at that very moment had an enterprise, a damage suit for nonexistent personal injuries, under way to provide him the funds to take advantage of the offer.

Reggie said he just claimed to be injured, there was no need to trouble "E'vis" up there in the sky, he was just fooling, to get the money for his teeth and to do something for his old parents and maybe have enough left over to get the engine rebuilt in his new car. I asked him why a brand new car needed to have the engine rebuilt and his father answered, saying Reggie must have bought a lemon because it was already using more oil than it did gasoline and the service manager at the dealer in Texarkana had said they would probably have to rebuild the engine. It would cost Reggie about a thousand dollars since it was not in the warranty.

I looked at Morales and he looked at me and we both realized that service manager was pulling a fast one on Reggie, that there was probably a simple reason why the car was using oil, something the dealer would repair in about five minutes time at no cost to him and for which he would charge Reggie all the traffic would bear. I told Reggie and the old man my associate Mr. Pittman was an experienced auto mechanic, which he was, having worked in the auto repair shop at Angola State Prison most of the time he was there, and he would be glad to look at the car and see if he could not fix it, and I noticed even that small a promise, that slight a hope, brightened the faces of all the Weed family.

Mizzrizz Weed called us in to supper and pointed out the bathroom in case we wanted to wash our hands. The bathroom had a wooden floor covered with linoleum which was rotten and spongy around the commode and under the basin. It would not do for me, a man who weighed just at three hundred pounds, to have to stand on that floor too long because I would just go right through it, a floor that water damaged and probably get trapped in among some studs on the foundation.

We all sat down at a round table in the kitchen, Mizzrizz Weed setting a place for all of us, even though she had no way of knowing we were not psychotic killers, planning to do them all in, which, come to think of it, the White River Kid was. He was behaving very well, almost relaxed and since I knew his pistol was still in the van, I was not worried about the possibility he might notice wooly gums in the eyes of his soon to be father-in-law or his almost brother-in-law Reggie, although I had no positive feelings about Reggie, whom I considered a common swindler and even less positive feelings about Lawyer Bearclaws, who was abetting his broken-back and damaged-lung scam. I thought that if the White River Kid, in his wisdom, ever saw wooly gums in the eyes of Reggie Weed and did what he could to release them, it would be no more of an outrage to society than it was when he released J. C. Bunn.

The Kid looked comfortable for the first time since I had met him, here among the Weed family at dinner. It was the family he had never had, it may have been just the thing he needed to get over his belief in wooly gums and get on the road to acting like a normal person, although I knew he was not likely to get away from justice in the matter of those six or eight he had killed and that law officers were looking for him right now. And I'm going to have to admit that I felt good at the Weed table, myself. I, too, felt like it was my family, a family I never had either, all my close relatives being dead and me being an only child. Here I was, not yet sixty years old with no blood relatives on earth but my Uncle Lillian, who lived in Dallas where he had worked for thirty years at a country club and who, when he was young, was known as the LBJ of lawn tennis, and a second cousin, a dress designer known as Lucille of Shreveport, who was now executive director of something called the Mable Dodge Mays Foundation for Young Women, a home for unwed mothers, I think it is, both distant relations and both highly respectable, people who would be embarrassed if I drove my van up in their driveway. So I pretended the Weeds were my family, like I felt the White River Kid must be doing, and I ate a big dinner, two plates of Uncle Ben's Rice with cream gravy and three pieces of salt meat, and when Mizzrizz Weed brought out the dessert, hot corn bread with Karo Syrup poured over it, I ate two pieces and I could tell she was pleased, even if nooky, that a man was at her table, and enjoying what she had fixed.

After supper, Mizzrizz Weed stayed in the kitchen cleaning up the supper dishes but the rest of us went out on the porch and sat down, some in the swing and some on the steps. Old man Weed noticed those bandages on the Kid's face and said something about how he looked like he had been "rasslin'" a bobcat. I could see the Kid was a little uneasy and did not know what to say, but about that time Apple Lisa came out on to the porch and grabbed the Kid's hand and said she wanted to show him the pond and the two of them left, walking across a field next to the house in the direction of a grove of trees I could see about two hundred yards away.

The old man and I sat in the swing, in the twilight. I pointed to the sorry-looking old minnow buckets and rabbit hutches in the front yard and asked him if it was true, what his wife had said, that he had not ever sold a single one of them. He said it was true, he had never sold a one, but every now and then, someone slipped up at night and stole one of them, which proved to him there was a market for his merchandise, if he could just hold out until it developed.

Mizzrizz Weed came out on the porch, drying her hands on a dish towel and asked her husband where "Liser" was and he said she had gone off to the pond with "that boyfriend of hers." Mizzrizz Weed snorted contemptuously, as if she knew why Apple Lisa had taken the White River Kid to a secluded grove two hundred yards away. I knew why she took him away, I knew what they were doing, just about now, they were making love, fucking, as they called it, two young people with smooth, perfect bodies, even if the Kid was sort of rat faced and even if Apple Lisa did look more like a sheep in the face than most young girls you run into, two youngsters, entwined in the grass alongside a quiet pond, under the trees, screwing like normal people, with no deviations, no hang-ups, no need for fan belts and hair brushes and high heeled boots. The thought of it filled me with sadness, not for Apple Lisa and the Kid, but for me, old Brother Edgar, three hundred pounds, if an ounce, old and out of it, the innocent lust of those two on the grass by the pond, forever gone.

Mrs. Weed, as I am now going to start calling her, asked me if we would like to stay there that night and I said we would, if it was no trouble and if they had enough room. She said it was no trouble and there was room enough, if some of the boys doubled up and right away Reggie said that Morales Pittman could sleep with him and Morales said something in a combination of Spanish and German, something like *"Bueno, wonderbar!"* that meant it would be all right with him.

She still had on that costume, Mrs. Weed did, and she said she hoped it would not keep us awake, but she stayed up most of the night, singing and dancing to Elvis Presley records, as a means of paying homage to him for having cured her cancer, and I said it would be no bother at all, although the thought I would have to listen to her sing while I was trying to go to sleep struck me as being in the same boat with the pain I once suffered in North Little Rock, Arkansas, when I had to stop my car right on the street, run behind a billboard, and stay there until I passed a kidney stone.

Old Man Weed told me there was no place for tourists to stay in Block Island and that the occasional stranger who came to town and wanted to stay the night had to go over to Prince a'Peace, Texas, eight miles away, where there was a motel, the only one in that part of the state. On the other hand, he said, there was no cafe in Prince a'Peace and that anyone there wanting a meal had to come to Block Island, to Dedley's Cafe, home of the Dedley Burger.

We sat on the porch until it was dark, until you could see bats flying around. Elvis Weed, the eleven-year-old boy, went out in the yard and threw small rocks up in the air and we watched the bats chase the falling rocks almost right to the ground, thinking they were bugs, something to catch and eat. After about two hours, Apple Lisa and the White River Kid showed up, walking out of the darkness into the light from the fifty-watt bulb in the porch ceiling and Old Man Weed said it must be about time to turn in and so we all went in the house, into the heat of an oven, and Mrs. Weed said there was a good breeze blowing in the back of the house. She told me I could sleep on the sofa in the living room and she put the White River Kid in with Elvis Weed and Reggie in with Morales Pittman. Apple Lisa had a cot in the hall and Mr. and Mrs. Weed had a bedroom in the back, where the good breeze was blowing. We had all settled in, we were all pouring sweat from the hot summer night, sleep was coming to us, when the lights in the kitchen went on, and I heard the voice of Elvis Presley singing some gospel number and soon Mrs. Weed joined him, singing at the top of her voice and I could see her dancing, twisting, her hands over her head. In spite of the distractions, I fell asleep but was awakened about thirty minutes later when a big dog, whose existence I had been unaware of, whom I had not seen since arriving at the Weeds' house, jumped up on the sofa with me. Mrs. Weed was still in the kitchen, gyrating and singing, so I got up and went outside to the van, opened the back doors and the front door and got in one of the bunks and tried to go to sleep again, but the mosquitoes were too bad, they were everywhere, I even breathed in one, right into a nostril, which gave me a fit of tickling and by the time I had blown it out and rubbed my nose until it stopped tingling, I was wide awake.

I saw the front door of the house open and the White River Kid came out, on the porch, wearing only a pair of jockey shorts. He walked out to the van and called my name in a whisper, "Brother Edgar! Brother Edgar! You in there?"

"Here I am, Kid! What's the matter? Anything wrong?"

The Kid shook his head, meaning nothing wrong, or so I took it to mean, and then he said, "I want to get shed of it."

"Shed of what, Kid?" I asked. The Kid touched his face, touched the butterfly and I knew what he meant. "You want to get the butterfly taken off your face?" He nodded. "Okay, Kid, tomorrow, we'll go see the doctor!" The Kid looked stone faced at me awhile, then turned and walked back to the house. I stayed in the van a minute, fighting the mosquitoes. Then I too went back into the house, into the living room and noticed the old lady had quit singing, she was passed out in a chair, so I turned off the record player, turned out the light, went back to the sofa, gave that big dog a good kick in the slats and got rid of him, and lay down and went to sleep.

E I G H T

Mrs. Weed came to in the kitchen about five-thirty the next morning and turned on the record player. This time it was Elvis Presley singing "You Ain't Nothing But a Hound Dog" and she sang along with him and danced after a fashion while she fixed breakfast for all of us. At about seven, she went around waking everyone up and calling them in to the table in the kitchen, where she served us each a big plate of grits, with a glob of margarine melting in the center of it, and a cup of hot coffee. These people, the Weeds, were as poor as any I had ever seen and from the looks of their house and the worn-out furniture in it, they could not afford to keep on feeding us like this without some help. I knew I had to give them some money, sooner or later, if we were going to stay there, and my plan for the Kid and the removal of his butterfly required we have a place for him to stay while his face healed. I did not want them to know I had quite a lot of money on me and more hidden in the van, because I did not want to tempt them to kill us all and steal it, an act that I did not put one inch past that brother of Apple Lisa's, the one with no front teeth, named Reggie.

After picking at a second helping of grits and drinking three cups of coffee with lots of sugar and lightened with Pet Milk from a can on the table, I got up and walked out of the house, through rooms with ceilings badly damaged by rain, and out to the van to check it and see if there had been any attempt to get inside of it during the night. When I found everything all right, I walked up the street two blocks to the main drag of Block Island, where I remembered seeing a little gas station and grocery store, where I might find a telephone so I could call Doc Poole in Hot Springs and make an appointment to bring the Kid in to have his butterfly removed.

The store was open and I found a pay telephone, got long distance information, found the Doc's home telephone number and called him, charging the call to my home telephone in Benton, Arkansas. Doc Poole remembered me right away, and when I told him I had a little "scar" I wanted him to remove, he knew I was talking about something outside the usual ethics of the medical profession and he got sort of conspiratorial with me, talking out of the corner of his mouth, like people did in gangster movies of the thirties. He said to come on in that afternoon, about four-thirty and he would see me last, when all the other patients were gone.

I hung up and then bought a honey bun from the girl in the store, and a bottle of chocolate milk and stood there, eating a little second breakfast, making small talk with her as she watched the morning news on television. I was thinking to myself, I wonder if there is any chance she might be looking for a little action, on a commercial basis, of course, since I had no illusions that, at nearly sixty years of age, and weighing as much as I do, I could get her to go along just for the thrill, when the man on television, the anchor man, as they call themselves, started talking about the White River Kid and reported that he had slipped through yet another trap set by sheriff's deputies outside Plumrod's Cafe in Como, Arkansas, two nights ago. "Authorities," said the television man, believed the Kid was still in the area but admitted that capturing him would be difficult since he knew the White River bottomlands better than anyone else and could find many places to hide, in addition to being able to live off the land.

That was all the television had to say about the Kid, no mention of me, my van, Morales Pittman, or Apple Lisa, the waitress who disappeared from the cafe at the same time the Kid did. I did not think it was a trick, not mentioning my van, or the deputies having questioned me about the Kid, I believed the "authorities" had no idea the Kid had help, but assumed he was still up there in northwest Arkansas, hiding in a pool of seep water, alongside a ten-foot gar and half a dozen water moccasins. I watched the news until it was over, hoping to hear something about the Bunn brothers, late of Socrates, Texas or Arkansas, but I heard nothing, meaning most likely, the Bunn brothers' remains, if any, had not yet been discovered.

I walked back to the Weed house, and gave Mrs. Weed twenty dollars, which I told her was to help pay for our stay. She took it and said she was much obliged, then said that twenty dollars would not go far, especially the way I ate. I apologized and said I had sold my watch to a man up at the settlement on the highway and that was all I could get for it and old man Weed's ears pricked up and he said he did not know there was anyone in Block Island who had twenty dollars, which I did not follow up on, but I told Mrs. Weed that I was going to have to take the Kid to the doctor this morning, for treatments for his face, and that I thought I could get some more money to help her out from a friend I had in Hot Springs.

Morales and Reggie were out in the front yard, looking at Reggie's new car which was burning oil at a greater rate than it was burning gasoline. I took Morales aside and told him I was taking the Kid to Hot Springs that morning to get that butterfly taken off his face and that I would be back late that night. When Reggie was not looking, I slipped him a few bills, no more than forty dollars, not because he needed money, because I knew Morales had just about every penny he had ever made working for me, but because I do not like to leave people who depend on me in strange places, without a little backup money. Morales took it and muttered something about *El Niño de Flumen Blanc* and *mariposa* and then he said *"Papillon finite"* which I could follow since I had been around him so long, but it was going to be hard for a stranger to make out what he was talking about.

The Kid had washed up in the Weeds' bathroom, with its spongy, water-soaked floor, and his hair was slicked back. When I asked him if he was ready to go, he nodded his head and we left in the van, heading to Hot Springs, the Kid sitting in the seat opposite me.

I could tell the Kid was enchanted by all the new sights he saw, things that you or me would not look at twice, cows, barns, windmills were things he had not seen all that much, living as he had like a river rat, slipping along in the mud of the White River banks, in and out of caves along its way that he shared with turtles and snakes, always too busy looking for food or a warm place to stay on a cold night to notice one cow from another, although he did mention once along the way when we saw some cows that "you can get sweet milk from them, if you pull their tits." I could tell the Kid was happy, maybe for the first time in his life, his belly full of grits, a suitcase of new clothes in the van, a girlfriend back at Block Island, and it was the farthest thing from my mind that he might have another spell of seeing wooly gums and want to free them from their human forms with that pistol he had carried from the first time I met him, and, as I look back on it, if it could be said that there was ever one given moment when I realized that I was acting outside the law, and admitted it to myself without any excuses or reservations, it was now, as I drove the Kid to the man who was going to remove his one distinguishing feature.

Yes, I admitted it and accepted it, and what is more, Mr. District Attorney or Mr. Public Prosecutor, I had willed, I had deliberately positioned myself outside of society, I had thrown in with the Kid all the way, and I was determined to try to change him, to camouflage him, to help him vanish into the masses, and, if you have followed my narrative so far with any degree of concentration and attention, you will see that such behavior on my part should have been predicted, forecast, and expected, for if there is one thing I have tried to make clear it is that I have always been at odds with society, I have always been a man who played by his own rules, sometimes to the extent of actually being an outlaw, why and for what reasons, I will leave to the psychologists and sociologists to speculate on.

We were nearing Hot Springs and I started getting just as excited about it as I did when I was a boy of twelve, thirteen, and fourteen and would go there once a year with my aunt and uncle who lived in Little Rock, Arkansas, and who spent one week a year in a cabin on Lake Hamilton, three miles out of Hot Springs itself, an inlet called Burchwood Bay, and stayed in the same cabin each time, one of four identical ones built and operated by a wiry old man with three fingers missing on his right hand, named Mr. Hawbecker. I noticed your ears prick up when I said I had an aunt and uncle in Little Rock, and that is true, but there is no need to go into my family history to carry out this narrative, although some day the psychologists might want to look into my childhood, living with a mother who never read anything but *Photoplay* magazine, to see if there was a clue there as to why I turned out like I did. Suffice it to say, that for nearly four years, I lived in Little Rock, Arkansas, with my aunt and uncle and during that time, came to know and love Hot Springs as one of the most thrilling places to be in the universe, and keep in mind that I have seen such cities as Tokyo; Seoul, Korea; New Orleans; and Eureka Springs, Arkansas.

Many a Sunday morning, my uncle would say, about eight-thirty A.M., to his wife, my aunt, that he thought it would be a good idea to drive over to Hot Springs for lunch at Hammonds Oyster House and we would all take up the idea, and it would be done. Hot Springs was about fifty-two miles from Little Rock, but in those days the trip took three hours because the road was so narrow and full of twists and curves that any speed was impossible.

Once you got out of Little Rock about ten miles, the Hot

Springs highway became a fairyland to a culturally deprived boy from Romeo, Texas, with roadside stands every hundred yards, selling apple and cherry cider, chenille bedspreads, hung right out on clotheslines in the yards of houses along the highway, and plaster lawn ornaments and Hot Springs souvenirs, and here and there, off the highway, glimpses of mountains in the distance. You will have to understand that Hot Springs, with a population of about twenty thousand, was an international resort, famous for the thermal springs right in town, and the bathhouses that had been built over them, and there was a racetrack, Oaklawn Park, and a famous nightclub, the Belevedere Club, where Al Capone himself and other Chicago and New York gangsters, went for relaxation. We are talking about the 1940s before and during World War II, when there was professional gambling, of the sort now legal at Las Vegas, but which was illegal then in Arkansas, but out in the open, nonetheless. Hot Springs was a town where the laws were ignored on some matters such as gambling and prostitution, and where everybody was having a good time and that is why I liked it, even at the age of twelve, I knew it was my element.

We would arrive at the south end of the city, and the first landmark I would look for was Philipps Drive Inn, which had the best barbecue I had ever eaten up to that time, and spaghetti and chili and where my aunt and uncle would stop for supper on the way back to Little Rock after a Sunday in town. The next landmark I looked for was Oscar's Bakery, the biggest bakery I had ever seen with the most delicious assortment of pastries I had ever run into up to that time.

In those days, the main street, called Central Avenue, was lit up and open all through the day, all night, with many auction houses selling things like "Jean Harlow's Bulova watch" or "a pair of ormolu lamps once owned by Buster Keaton" and people sitting inside, half of them shills, keeping up a trade in such items. There were jewelry stores selling Hot Springs diamonds, zircons, really, but which looked real, and the restaurants, Hammonds Oyster House and the National Cafe were my uncle's favorites. Hammonds had the entire front open to the street and I have never until this moment, as I sat down to recall those days, thought about how they keep flies out of the place. My uncle went to Hammonds for Pompano en Papillote and I always got lemon meringue pie. There were great, grand hotels, the Arlington, the Majestic, and the Como, and upstairs over the shops on Central Avenue were the offices of the medical quacks, the unscrupulous healers who preyed on the elderly Jews from Chicago who flocked there, by offering electrotherapy for arthritis, and colonic irrigation as a treatment for anything that ails you.

There were strange houses, perched on mountainsides, and one of them was a replica of a Russian villa, with lots of colors and wooden trim unlike anything I had ever seen, and lots of places to gamble on sports, usually called cigar stores, and beer joints that opened at six-thirty in the morning. The entire city was corrupt, the mayor on down to the garbage collector, and after the war, a reform element got in power and changed the city in a lot of ways that did away with all the things I found exciting, but at the time I was going there for a week in the summer and about once a month on Sunday, it was unlike anything else in the whole United States of America.

As we got into town, I could tell the Kid was having the same reactions to Hot Springs as I did forty some years ago, except in the Kid's case, Hot Springs was not only a resort with hotels and shops, but it surely must have been the biggest town he had ever seen. When he saw those marble buildings called Bathhouse Row, eight stately structures of marble, stucco, and tile, with names like The Buckstaff, I could swear he must have thought he had died and gone to heaven, for never in his life had he ever seen or imagined such big, palatial, and opulent structures, as he was now seeing for the first time. I drove through town, from one end of it to the other, letting him get an eyeful then I drove back down Central Avenue and parked the van near the Arlington Hotel and we got out and walked across the street to the dining room of the Majestic Hotel, where we sat down and I ordered lunch for us, as the Kid's eyes were taking in everything new.

Speaking of his eyes, they did not know what to make of the rainbow trout he was served, since it had its head still attached, a way of serving fish not common in the circles where the Kid grew up. It did no good for me to explain that was how trout was served because he was raised too much of a wild boy to accept social conventions, such as a fish served at the table with its head still attached and he lost his appetite and did not eat anything, which was all right with me. I had not had anything to eat since that honey bun earlier in the morning, and it was no trouble for me to move the Kid's plate over to my place at the table and eat his trout as well as mine.

On the way into Hot Springs from Block Island, I had talked to the Kid about "going to the doctor," as I called our planned visit with my old friend Doc Dorris Poole, who was no doctor but who had lived as one several times that I knew about.

I learned that the Kid had never ever in his life, that he remembered, been to see a doctor or required any medical treatment and I was afraid he might get excited when Doc Dorris Poole started to remove that tattoo, fearful of the pain or of the unknown in general and go off on us, maybe getting violent and injuring somebody, although there was no danger of his shooting anyone with that pistol he usually carried because I had it safely tucked away in a box in the back of the van, and I tried to assure him there would be no pain, that the "doctor" would not hurt him and that when it was all over, the butterfly would be gone and there would no longer be any way the deputies could recognize him, and he seemed to understand and said he would go ahead with the removal, although I would rank the removal of that tattoo with the melting down of some piece of gold sculpture by Cellini, it was that much of a work of art and it made me wish I could get hold of that tattoo artist, find out if he was still alive, and maybe start managing him, selling his work to the color magazines, if it were possible.

It was about two o'clock when we left the Majestic Hotel, nearly two and a half hours before we were supposed to be in Doc Poole's office and so I started walking the Kid along Central Avenue, looking at the sights. It is one thing to pass a row of shops in a car or a van, and still another to actually walk along the sidewalk in front of them, because you can see so many more details, and it was the details in the shop windows that now fascinated the Kid, such things as a ball and powder pistol in a pawn shop window, antique flintlock rifles and mounted heads of wild animals, bobcats, deer, and wolves, and new clothes, men's suits, shoes, and straw hats in the clothing stores, ladies' dresses on mannequins, cafe windows with cuts of watermelon on beds of crushed ice in them, and pyramids of fruit, cantaloupe, oranges, lemons stacked in geometrical arrangements.

By the time we had walked the length of the business district on Central Avenue and back again, the Kid was worn out from the strain of taking in new sights and concepts and I would venture to say that he learned more about the world in that afternoon, just from looking at things he had never seen before, than in all the rest of his young life.

I had been talking to the Kid all along the way, trying to reassure him about what was going to happen in Doc Poole's office and by the time we were actually ready to go there, the Kid was so tired I was convinced he would cooperate and sit still as Dorris Poole started to work on him.

The Doc's office was on Central Avenue, upstairs over a pawn shop and next door to a kosher restaurant, and there was a sign over the doorway that said:

D. E. POOLE

PHYSICAL THERAPY
COLONIC IRRIGATION
FOOT MASSAGE

"D. E. Poole" was Dorris Eugene Poole. There ought to be some way to severely punish a parent who would name a male child Dorris Eugene Poole, even if Dorris was spelled with two r's, or who would name a son Beverly or Ruby or Evelyn, because people live up or down to their names. What hope does a boy named Dorris have of living up to anything, when he gets laughed at by other boys every day of his life and dismissed as a sissy by boys and girls too, and is lucky if he does not grow up a song leader with a Bible act, or maybe a floral designer?

We walked up the steep stairs, which were covered with worn-through linoleum, to a doorway at the top with a frosted glass pane and the words OFFICE—ENTER lettered on it. The door opened into a small room where about eight people were waiting, in an atmosphere that smelled of linament and raw sewage.

It all looked pretty seedy, worn-out fixtures in the waiting room, more worn linoleum on the floor, cracked plaster walls, an old Coca-Cola advertisement, Santa Claus, with his hat off, refreshing himself with a Coca-Cola after a hard night of delivering presents to the world's good little boys and girls, being the only ornament on the walls.

You might think my old friend Doc Poole was to be pitied, ending up like this, practicing some vague ministry in the health field, in the shabbiest of surroundings. But if you knew as much about him as I do, you would be proud of him for having come back from the bottom of the pit with even this much going for him, for Doc Poole, whom I first met when we were both young and living in New Orleans, had about the worst drug habit I had ever seen in my life.

He wound up in Hot Springs in his present situation about three years ago and seems to be happy and able to make enough money out of it, not counting what he made removing tattoos and bullet scars from various members of the criminal element.

The Kid was relaxed, sitting in the waiting room, looking at a magazine and I looked at those in the waiting room, "reading" them, as an old con man will automatically do.

There were two young black men, each about twenty-five, one of whom was there to see Doc Poole about "a growth on de ball de foot"; a fat countrywoman about thirty, wearing purple pants that were almost splitting out, and her daughter, a beautiful little girl of about twelve; another woman, about fifty, who had her arm in a sling, who had brought in her son, a man about thirty, who made a living working underneath automobiles, one of those whose shoes are always drenched in brake fluid and who was destined to be crippled one day when the jack slipped. He was there to see the Doc because his knee had "give" on him. I listened to the snatches of conversation, picking up bits here and there. For instance, I heard one of the black men say "I bee's drunk, but I don't bee's out my mine!" a reference to his condition when stopped recently at the wheel of an automobile by the city police officers, and I heard the other one later ask him, "Do de dog be foam at de mouf?" a reference to a pit bull that lived near the other and who menaced him whenever he stepped out in his yard. Doc Poole has always been very fond of the black man and I can remember one time in New Orleans, when a gang of us were in the bar at Tujague's on Decatur, back in the early sixties, back when we white liberals used to vie with each other to express our sympathy with the blacks in their fight for civil rights, one of those present accused Doc Poole of not liking black people and the doc got hot about it and said, "Don't tell me I don't love blacks! Why the first time I ever got fucked in the ass it was by a black man!" and that was true, I knew it for a fact, because I was with Doc the night he met him. In those days, we would sometimes go to the City Night Court, just to see misery we were not involved in, maybe that, maybe just to learn about life, and one night Doc and I were there and heard the bailiff call out the next case, "Sampson Dillard!" and Sampson Dillard appeared. He was a huge black man, some sort of dock worker, doubtless, a stevedore, strong enough to lift a bale of cotton, probably, and he was wearing a pink dress and pink high heel shoes and carrying a pink chiffon scarf, but he had lost his wig. When Doc Poole saw him, standing there at the mercy of some mafioso judge, he felt sympathetic and the upshot was, he stepped up and paid his fine, with thirty dollars he was planning to use to buy dope. Dillard was surprised and grateful and took us home to where his friend, Morgan, lived. Morgan was another black man, who was a disc jockey on a New Orleans radio station, and he was the black man Doc was talking about, the one he first got together with. Doc hung around him a long time, because being a disc jockey, he was always being given dope by the record promoters, and since he did not use it, and as far as I was ever able to tell, had no bad habits whatever, he gave it to Doc and he and Doc got to be in pretty thick, which made Sampson Dillard, who incidentally, was not a dock worker, but a window trimmer at the Bon Marché, very jealous.

The two black men in the waiting room were sharing a confidence, one was whispering in the other's ear and the receiver of the confidence said to the other, "My lips be seal!" just as the door to the waiting room opened and a woman about sixty, with a hardened country face, came in, leading a boy about eight, who ran away from her to the far end of the waiting room as soon as she let go his hand, causing her to say, "You get back over here and set down, Paul Newman the Third!"

The boy sat down, next to the old woman, who was moving with some difficulty, and I presumed she was there to see Doc Poole about some problem with her spine, maybe to have it snapped back into place. The two black men were talking about some girl they both knew and how pretty she was and how, one time, one of them was out with her and how "de moon be shine" when they walked down Central Avenue. The old lady with her arm in a sling, the mother of the auto mechanic, asked the fat young mother of the twelve-year-old girl what she had come to see the doctor for and the woman said, "Doctor Poole said Verssie Lee ain't got no circulation in her toes. He said if they ain't no better soon, he may have to lave them." The woman with her arm in a sling asked what "laving" was and the fat mother said, "Doc Poole said it was an old Indian remedy and that if he can't find an old Indian to do it, he may have to do it himself."

When I heard that, it was all I could do to keep a straight face, I mean, I nearly fell out of my chair laughing inside, to myself. I envisioned the scene, the lovely child, on her back on a treatment table, with a some sort of screen across her chest, so she could not see what the doctor was doing to her feet, and Doc Poole, down on his knees, holding those little toes in his mouth with one hand while he beat off with the other and it occurred to me that that was a perfect example of what all therapy, mental and physical, amounts to in the end.

The two black men had been talking about salvation and human perfection and one of them said to the other, in reply to how many people on earth will get to heaven, "Ain't nobody is!"

Finally, all the other patients were seen, the little girl's toes were laved, the mechanic's knee was packed in bandages soaked in liniment, the growth on the black man's foot was pared down, and the little boy was treated for a case of Palmer's Crotch, a fungus infection, which I could hear the old woman, his grandmother, as it turned out, telling Doc Poole had been caused by the boy's constant "playing with hisself!" I pitied that poor boy with all my heart, having to put up with crap like that from a half-crazy old ignoramaus of a grandmother, and wished I could free him and every other poor son of a bitch on earth from meddling authority figures. When everyone else was out of the waiting room, Doc Poole came out from the examining room, locked the outside door, and shook hands with me. I had not seen him in ten years, but we had kept in touch, and so I started in right away, kidding him about his old Indian treatment and he laughed and said for a minute he thought the child had seen him whacking off, but it was apparently a false alarm. Then he shook hands with the Kid, who had been sitting still in the chair like a little man all the time we had been there, and did not appear to be the least fidgety or nervous.

We went inside to the Doc's examination room and he put the Kid in a chair something like a dentist's chair and turned on a light that lit up the tattoo on his cheek. Doc Poole looked at it a minute and then said to me, without turning around to face me, "There are some people up in northwest Arkansas right now looking for a man with a tattoo like this on his cheek. They say they are going to call out the National Guard to find him, to comb those swamps, if they don't catch him soon." I gave the Doc a noncommittal answer and he said he would have to have a hundred dollars, old friends or not, to remove this particular tattoo.

I told the Doc to go ahead, that I had that kind of money on me and it would be no problem, so he sat the Kid down good in the chair and then washed his left cheek with a soapy iodine solution, then rewashed it, and dried it with cotton held in some sort of tongs. He took out a hypodermic needle and told the Kid he was going to give him a little shot so he would not feel the pain, and I assured the Kid it would not hurt because I knew the Kid had never had a shot of any kind and I did not want him to go off and start fighting the Doc. The Kid said to go ahead and so the Doc did, sticking the needle into his cheek at several places around the tattoo. When it was over the Kid just smiled and said it felt about the same as when a rat tried to bite your face when you are sleeping and I had such a pang of pity in my heart to hear the Kid actually suggest he had experienced rats in his bed at night, that I thought I was going to quit breathing.

The Doc puttered around a few minutes, waiting for the anesthetic to take effect and explained a little about his technique, which I had assumed was something he had developed himself, but after hearing him tell about it, I realized it was common, something done every day by dermatologists. It was called "dermabrasion" said the Doc and all it amounted to was to sort of sandpaper the tattoo right off the face. When he was sure the anesthetic had taken effect, he brought out a tank of some sort of gas, under pressure, and sprayed the tattoo with it, and right away, ice formed on the Kid's face. When the Doc asked me if I would like to feel the spot, and I did, and that part of the Kid's jaw where the tattoo was had been frozen solid, hard like a sheet of steel. The Doc then put a tiny wire brush into one of those things dentists put steel bits in to drill away cavities in your teeth and turned it on, and started brushing away the tattoo with it. He worked deftly, just the right pressure, just dusting away the surface, never going too deep, and flakes of frozen flesh flew all over the Kid's shoulder. There was no bleeding, all the blood vessels in the cheek had been frozen and the procedure was no different than a carpenter using a sanding wheel to brush away a slight imperfection on a hardwood surface.

In five minutes, the Doc was finished with the wire brush and he turned it off, set it aside, and opened a small tin of something he said he had mixed up himself, Vaseline, iodine, and sugar and spread it on the surface where the tattoo had been. I questioned him about the sugar. What did the sugar do? I asked, and he said sugar was the oldest antibiotic in the world, bacteria cannot form in sugar, he said, and while the iodine itself would prevent infection, the combination of iodine and sugar, something he called Sugardine, would make healing more rapid, and would leave no scar. He said it was his trade secret, the same that made those New York gangsters willing to pay his price to remove their distinguishing blemishes. He put a bandage on the Kid's face, told us the spot would thaw out at about the same rate that the blood would coagulate and there should not be any bleeding. He gave me a tin of Sugardine salve to take with me and said I was to rub the surface with it three times a day, massaging it in and he guaranteed it would heal as good as new in a week or ten days.

I paid Doc Poole his hundred dollars and the Kid and I left his office and started walking along Central Avenue, in the direction of the Arlington Hotel, near where we had parked the van, to head back to Block Island. It had been a long day for me and I knew the Kid must be tired, too, for just the excitement of seeing Hot Springs, Arkansas, had surely been enough to lay him out from exhaustion. A few yards from the van, I noticed a man standing by it, a large manila envelope in his hand, obviously waiting for the owner or driver to return. His presence there threw a scare into me at first, but after I had looked him over carefully, after I had "read" him, I knew he was no officer of the law. I walked up to him and before I could say anything, he said to me, "I am Kenrod Dreary, the Poet," and from his manner I could tell he expected me to be impressed, much the same as if he had been a real poet, like A. E. Housman, and, having dealt with crossroads poets for years, I knew how to respond, I said, "What a pleasure!" and he pointed to the line painted on the side of my van and said he wanted to enter some of his poems in the POETRY CONTEST.

You will recall I have mentioned that I purport to be an agent for a poetry contest, vaguely connected with The Little Brothers of St. Mortimer, and hinting that the winners will be immediately acclaimed the world over, and that I accept entries to the contest everywhere I stop and spend the day selling socks, although, in fact, there is no poetry contest, there will be no winners, and for that matter there is also no such thing as The Little Brothers of St. Mortimer, except as it exists in my imagination, and the only thing real about the contest is the five-dollar cash entry fee I accept from those wanting to enter their work. You might be surprised how many unpublished poets, or persons calling themselves poets, there are in the small towns of America, and how many of them are willing to invest five dollars in trying to get published or win prizes and fame, but it is a fact that, when I am really out working hard, traveling daily, hitting one town after another, I never take in less than fifty dollars a day in poetry entry fees, and the one thing I am most proud of, is, as far as I know, I am the only traveling sock salesman in the nation who is working this con, although, of course, there are many magazines and poetry societies who do it, but the difference between me and them is, they really do seem to have a contest and occasionally publish work that is submitted to them, although no one ever reads it, or could read it, if he tried.

I told Mr. Dreary that I would be happy to accept his entry and he then stated that he was the foremost poet in Garland County, Arkansas, where Hot Springs is located, and would not be surprised if he were not the best poet in the state, better even than Lindsey Windsong, a man who lived in Siloam Springs, Arkansas, who some said was another Dalton Blassingame, and whose works could be found in truck stops all over the state, printed on good rag paper, pasted to a small piece of plywood with a hole in the top of it to permit it to be hung on the wall, and then given a good coat of shellac. Mr. Dreary handed me about thirty or forty poems, each written on a separate sheet of paper and said he wanted to enter them all and I smiled and said to him, "You understand, of course, there is a slight entrance fee, which the Little Brothers of St. Mortimer apply to the medical expenses of those who cannot afford needed medical treatment," and I pointed to the Kid, who had been standing there all this time, tired and eager to get in the van and go to sleep on one of the bunks, and to the bandage on his face and I said, "For instance, we are here in Hot Springs today, to enable this young man have a skin cancer removed from his jaw and were it not for us, he would have no means to have this done and would end up with his jaw removed and having to take nourishment through a wheat straw."

Mr. Dreary said he quite understood and asked how much the fee would be to enter the poems he had handed me and I took them and looked at them. Ordinarily, I consider roadside poets to be sheep born to shear, although I occasionally run across an earnest young man who has just learned perhaps by chance that life is tragic, that men will go through life unappreciated and worked to death, that they will make bad marriages, that they will go blind, that their children will go to jail, that they will never have two thin dimes in their pocket and that they will die in pain, and hastens to warn his fellows of this through the medium of free verse and I am sometimes sympathetic and have been known to let such enter the poetry contest without paying an entrance fee, but in the case of Mr. Dreary, I would not be so disposed. Most of his poems were in praise of what he called the "helping occupations," forest rangers, tugboat captains, chartered accountants, firemen, parole officers, and the like, and I saw he had written about ten poems on the human thumb and a few more celebrating the existence of the lap dog.

I told him that, in view of the sizable number of poems he was entering, the fee would be twenty dollars and he took out his wallet and paid it over without any protest and I opened the door of the van and found an *Official Entry Blank* and asked him to fill it out and I told him to be sure to put in the address where he wanted the royalty check sent and he eagerly filled out the form and handed it back to me and I thought that would be the end of him but it was not, for he wanted to talk poetry to someone, anyone, even a fat old Brother, like me, and I listened to him because I understood he needed to talk to someone because there were no others in town who had any sense, who could even understand what he was trying to do, and I listened to him and I was patient, that is, until he asked me what was the poet's mission, and by that time I was getting tired and I knew the Kid was on the point of getting fretful and I wanted to tell him that I considered the poet's mission was to use rhyme and meter in his work but I did not because I did not want to throw in something I knew he had never heard of.

At last, I was able to shake Mr. Kenrod Dreary and the Kid and I got in the van. What was he? asked the Kid. A poet, I said. The Kid wanted to know what a poet was. How could I explain that to him when he did not even know what the days of the week were called. I tried to think of a word for poet that might help the Kid understand or which might help him get a handle on what a poet was. A poet is a man who plays with words, I said. Is that good? asked the Kid. Poets used to be good, I told him. In the old days some poets could play with words and put them down on paper and when you'd read them, you'd get goosebumps. There's none of them around now. Poets who can raise the goosebumps, that is.

What is a poet, the Kid asked me again. I thought of words that meant poet to me. Nuisance. Pest. I thought the word pest might be best to try on the Kid. Poets are pests, I said. Pests? I could see I was still far from explaining a poet to the Kid. They're sort of like bugs, I said. The Kid's face lit up. Like ticks! he said. Yes, Kid, I said, poets and ticks are about the same thing.

We drove a few miles until I came to one of those roadside parks and I stopped there, threw Mr. Dreary's poems into the trash can and drove on, an act which some of you might consider inexcusable. You're probably going to ask me why I didn't just keep his poems a year or two then return them to him with a rejection slip, like any poetry magazine would do, but I am not so inclined, for it has always been one of the cornerstones of my code of behavior, that short men and free-verse poets are to be treated unmercifully.

It was nearly six-thirty, I was tired and getting hungry, and Block Island, which the Kid was already calling "home," was nearly eighty miles away and it would be over two hours before we got there, before I could relax. And then it struck me, I, too, had begun to think of Block Island as home, the Weed house, run-down and ramshackle as it was, hot as an oven at night, the floor in the bathroom rotten, was where I wished I was right now. I had only known them two days, but I realized I had grown fond of Baker Weed and his wife, dressed up all the time to look like Elvis Presley, and that is where I wanted to be, Baker Weed's house in Block Island, sitting down to whatever supper Mrs. Weed had been able to put together, and then to be able to go out on the porch and sit there with the Weeds, Baker, his wife, that worthless son Reggie, the neurotic son Elvis Weed, and Apple Lisa, and drift in and out of sleep before it was time to go inside, kick the dog off the sofa, and go to bed. The comforts of home, such things are called and that is what I suddenly longed for, a home, a family to share troubles with, and it came to me from nowhere, that not only had the Kid found a family, after over twenty years of being kicked around and living wherever he could, but I had too, and I felt good about it, felt good about being Brother Edgar, felt good about my future, for the first time in a long while.

NINE

When we got to Block Island, it was after dark, but the Weed family was on the porch waiting for us. When the Kid got out of the van, Apple Lisa was there to take him by the hand and lead him off in the darkness, to be together, I would guess, and old Baker Weed, he was smiling to see me, sort of the same way I was smiling to see him, because I could tell he liked me, too, and I knew I was welcome in his house, if for no other reason than I was somebody new to talk to, someone who had not yet heard all he had to say. Mrs. Weed was there, too, still in her Elvis Presley costume, rocking in the darkness, because she had turned out all the lights in the house since light bulbs create heat and no one wanted any extra heat inside that house when it came time to go to bed. She said to me that there was some beans and wieners on the stove in the kitchen if I was hungry and I started in to fix me a plate, telling Baker I would be right back out and eat supper there on the porch with him, when Elvis Weed, that pitiful little boy with a multitude of neuroses obvious to any layman, all caused I would guess by the fact his mother had named him after Elvis Presley, and was always after him to do Elvis impressions, and who expected him to grow up like Elvis did, to have long, greasy hair that he kept dyed to look like a Cherokee Indian and who would be good to his mother, grabbed my hand and said something that was the best news I could ever hope to hear, "Two men got eat up by hogs!"

I knew right away what he was talking about, he was talking about those two worthless Bunn brothers who me and Morales Pittman had dragged off the highway, as deep into the woods as we had the strength to drag them, to lay them right in the path where I hoped and prayed the hogs would get them, clean up every bit of evidence, so there would never be any chance of some sharp country town prosecutor, who wanted to be governor, rigging up a way to try me for the murder of those two "upstanding" citizens so he could get some publicity. But I had to play like I did not know what he was talking about and I asked him, "What two men, son? You say two men got eat by hogs? Well, how in the world could something like that happen?"

Baker Weed started in to explain, he said it was two fellows from over at Socrates, he also pronounced it SO-crates, Houston and J. C. Bunn, two sons of bitches who somehow managed to pass out a ways off the road, in amongst a pack of Razorback hogs, who must have just eat up every bit of them, because the marshal was not able to find a single trace of their bodies. I had to pretend like all this was news to me, that, in fact, the possibility that two grown men might ever be eaten entirely by wild hogs was something I had never heard of. I pressed Baker Weed for more facts and he said they heard it on the noon news on television, a channel out of Texarkana, Rob Boone, Jr., anchorman, who reported that the marshal at Socrates, a man named Ben T. "I Love Puppies" Newsome, had been on patrol on the road out of Socrates and had come upon the pickup truck of the Bunn brothers, parked off the side of the road, the doors open, the keys in the ignition, but no sign of the Bunn brothers.

The marshal said he started looking around in the under-brush near the truck and came upon a trampled area, where there was evidence of ten to fifteen wild hogs, rooting and snorting around, and he saw dried blood on some of the bushes and on some leaves on the ground and concluded that the Bunn brothers had got out of their truck for some reason, had gone into the woods, again for unknown reasons, and were there jumped by the hogs, who killed them and ate the bodies as well as the boots and clothes. Baker Weed told me all he had heard on television, along with the statements of some of the people of Socrates, including a man who clerked at the store in town, this would be that ex-schoolteacher, the one who could not keep a job for pawing the boys, who described the Bunn brothers as "pure D angels" and who said the community had lost two outstanding men.

Then another man told the story as he had imagined how it happened and I could tell he knew the Bunn brothers for the rats they were, because he guessed that one of them took the other off the road to kill him, maybe for no more than the change in his pockets, and things went wrong and the both of them got killed, or maybe, he speculated, it was a double sui-cide, the Bunn brothers having maybe got religion and realizing how trashy they were, how just generally no count, they had decided to end it all. I asked Baker Weed how well he knew the Bunn brothers and he said they stole a minnow bucket or a rabbit hutch from his inventory out there in the front yard every time they came that way, and they had not a single use for minnow buckets because they were strictly bottom fisher-men and no need for rabbit hutches because they were both allergic to fur, they just took away his property for meanness. He was not a bit sorry that the Lord had put them in the path of a herd of wild hogs, to see that His justice was done.

I breathed a little easier, I do not mind telling you, although I realized there was a complication I had not been aware of when I planted those two bodies in the woods, and that was the ex-schoolteacher back in Socrates, that storekeeper. He knew the Bunn brothers had set out to waylay us a little bit up the road and my only hope was the possibility he thought in his own mind that the Bunn brothers had in fact gotten us, that it was our blood the marshal, that "I Love Puppies" fellow, had seen and that the Bunn brothers were off somewhere in our van. I relaxed. I said to myself, let him think that, let him if he will, for I knew there was never the slightest chance of his realizing we had overcome the Bunn brothers, because I was at pains while in his store to make it look like I was just a sissy ass old Brother and the two boys, The Kid and Morales Pittman were effete, unmanly missionaries of some sort, the three of us being the last combination in his eyes ever to best the Bunn brothers.

So it looked like I had been lucky again, that there wasn't going to be any trouble, that I had squeezed out of another mess, and I looked around for Morales Pittman to tell him about it, to share our good luck with but he was not to be seen, and I asked Baker Weed where he was, and he said "gone." I looked out in the yard, where Reggie's new car had been parked when I left Block Island early that morning, and it was gone and Reggie was not there either. Weed handed me a note and said that Morales Pittman had asked him to give it to me when I returned and I opened it and read what amounted to a farewell note from Morales Pittman, good-bye forever, it said in essence. In a combination of languages that was harder to read than his spoken language was hard to understand, Pittman said that if I would rather have the White River Kid, or *El Niño de Flumen Blanc* as he put it, as a friend than him, that was all right with him, and good-bye forever.

Baker Weed must have read my face, even in the light of that forty-watt light bulb I had turned on in the house to read the note, he must have seen that I was hurt, cut by Morales Pittman's unfounded jealousy, and he said, "Reggie's gone, too. They went off together." Baker Weed explained that Morales had found out what was wrong with Reggie's new car, why it was leaking oil, and had repaired it easily, since all it amounted to was a cap unscrewed, probably deliberately by the mechanics at the auto dealer's, as a way to justify an expensive engine repair, and now that his car was working perfectly, Reggie and

Morales had run off together to Dallas, Texas, a place where Reggie had high hopes of making a lot of money suing people for personal injuries and damages, since he had read about a man in Dallas who had been awarded one million dollars when he sued an amusement park for selling him a bad hot dog which caused his insides to knot up.

Baker Weed thought that was all there was to it, Reggie moving on out to where the big judgments were and Morales Pittman going along just to get to Dallas, but I knew more about Morales Pittman than he did, in fact, I knew all about him, and I also had read Reggie, made him, as a carnival man would, knew what was inside him, just by looking at him, a talent I had developed from having had to do it right the first time, to stay out of hot water, for many years. It was a real mistake to allow those two to spend the night in the same bed together, Morales Pittman being fond of what I knew he was fond of, and Reggie, a repressed homosexual, isolated in a closed society, the social structure of Block Island, all his life, never realizing, never even dreaming there was anyone else in the world who had the same urges he had. What he must have always considered the most unattainable of all his dreams came true, he was put in a bed for the night with Morales Pittman, a man who had experienced everything there was to do, a man who had once even been involved in an orgy with a roomful of veterinarians at a convention in Waco, Texas, that ended with everyone getting off while watching an Indian princess named Mary Bearskin shit on a collie.

It was a real mistake, on my part that is, to let such a pair go to bed; Morales Pittman, vexed with me for my interest in the White River Kid (which as you should have been able to perceive was strictly paternal and should not have been any cause of concern to him), jealous, hurt, maybe vengeful, ready to get even with me; and Reggie, dreaming for years of just such an opportunity coming his way, the chance to go to bed with another man.

I made a mistake, I should have been able to see what was coming, after all, I have been telling you how good I am at knowing about people, about what they are really thinking and feeling, and here I have let myself be, well, maybe hurt a little, when I should have been able to foresee what was coming and prevent it, but, what is done is done.

I bear no grudges, and never have and it has always been my deepest belief that everything works out for the best. If I had had the chance, and Morales Pittman had come up to me and said he was jealous of the White River Kid, and besides had accidentally run up on something a lot more fun than what he was used to, someone much younger and with a lot more stamina, and wanted to go off to Dallas, Texas, with him, I would have given him my blessing and that would have been all there was to it.

I am not a man who expects things to last, who thinks that anything is permanant, and it would have been no surprise to me, no shock, for Morales to tell me he wanted to leave with Reggie. The only regret I have about what has developed, apart from being deprived of the company of Morales Pittman, whom you will agree had done me a lot of favors in the past, whom you might say had even saved my life, was the fact that I could not have said good-bye to him and let him know I understood what had upset him, but I am not going to dwell on that either, for neither do I bear a grudge nor dwell overlong on what might have been.

I took my plate of beans and wieners out on the front porch and sat in the darkness with Baker Weed and Mrs. Weed and we talked softly as the crickets or cicadas chirped in the woods nearby. They asked about the Kid and how the treatment for his cancer of the face went and I told them the doctor said he got it all, which is what doctors always tell you, even when they have just opened up a chest, seen what was there, what rot was eating away at some poor son of a bitch's life, and then sewed it back up again, and they were happy to hear that the Kid was going to be all right.

Baker Weed said Apple Lisa has asked him to take the Kid into his business and he had told her he would, since the Kid was going to be his son-in-law.

I told Baker Weed and his wife how glad I was to know them and how much I liked staying there and asked if it would be all right for me to stay another week or ten days and I said I would give them fifty dollars to pay for what I ate and what the Kid would eat and they were glad to accept the offer and Mrs. Weed even said I did not have to worry about paying anything to stay there, that since I was the Kid's people, which was her way of saying she thought I was related to the White River Kid, soon to be her son-in-law, and therefore, also family to be, that I did not have to pay.

What she said made me sort of cry, a little. When I learned Morales Pittman had run off with Reggie, I felt low. I do not mind telling you, I felt low and sad and down-and-out but I forgot about that, I forgot about Morales, when Mrs. Weed said I was "family."

I felt very close to the Weeds then and as I thought about them, I began to get depressed all over again, thinking about the bleakness of their lives.

I do not know exactly how long the Weeds had been married but I would guess they got married after Baker Weed got back from Korea, which would have been about 1954, and if that was true, then they had been married over thirty-five years and as far as I could determine they had lived in that same house all the time, a house they still rented from a man in Block Island who was described as "the arrogant Hugo Marfeedian, former Syrian lapidary," by the Weeds every time they mentioned him, and I never found out if it was some sort of private joke or in fact an exact characterization of the man, but I did know from their stories of dealing with him that he was utterly ruthless when it came to collecting the rent and about twice a year threatened to set them out in the street because it was late.

I do not think they had ever had an automobile, or that they had ever been far from Block Island although Baker Weed once did tell me that Mrs. Weed, who he said "was distantly related to the filthy rich," once made a trip to Texarkana on the bus to attend a funeral of a old aunt, a woman the Weeds still referred to as "Easter Lillian" for reasons I never learned, who had died "from eating peeled banana" which remained another mystery to me.

The Weeds had no air conditioner, not even a window fan, and in the winter that drafty house was heated by little "chill chasers," natural gas heaters that sent a blue flame up into ceramic coils and looked pretty on a cold night and made a reassuring, hissing sound. They had an old radio in a cracked Bakelite case which was kept in the kitchen and they had a television set, an old Admiral, black and white, with a small screen and a rabbit ear aerial that was broken and augmented with a piece of metal foil wrapped around the end of each ear. They did not get any newspapers, they never got a single letter the whole time I was there, they had only one caller, a thin old woman with dyed hair, who used to walk up into the yard about once a day, stand looking at me and Baker Weed on the porch, gazing at us without blinking an eye for as long as twenty minutes at a time then say to the both of us, "If the President of the United States knew what was going on here, he would get out a writ," then she would leave, returning to her own house.

I asked Baker Weed about the woman and he said she was Mrs. Shellnut, who had been married to Midas Shellnut for twenty years and who had made his life a hell on earth by her constant nagging and bossing him around and then one time, Midas got away from her to go to Malvern, Arkansas, to attend his twentieth high school reunion and there he ran into an old high school sweetheart who was now a widow and she and Midas hit it off right then and there, and Midas never came back to Block Island and I thought about that a minute and I said, with some tears in my eyes, that that was the sweetest story I had ever heard and Baker, tears in his eyes, sort of, anyway, said he thought so too.

The Weeds watched television most nights, Baker Weed bringing the old set out on the porch and plugging it into an outlet in the front room with a long extension cord. They never watched anything but situation comedies and sometimes they would remark on how funny the audience thought this or that

1 3 8

crack was and I never told them the truth, that the laughter they heard was fake, canned, turned on at the press of a button by someone in a dark room operating a computer and that the actual people whose voices were recorded had all been dead since the 1950s, at least, for such would have just disturbed them.

At least once a night, Baker would point to some actor or actress on a show and ask Mrs. Weed if that was a nigger and she would say yes, and Baker would ask why it was there were so many niggers on television and Mrs. Weed would say it was because the government made them put niggers on television and Baker Weed would say, what I'd like to know is when is the government going to do something for the white man.

The Weeds had lived almost all their lives without ever hearing of or seeing the entertainers that had made my life more enjoyable and whom I was thankful I had lived to see, people like Maurice Chevalier, Milton Berle, Lotte Lenya, Greta Keller, I could go on and on, but on the other hand, I had never seen or heard any of the entertainers who had made their lives more enjoyable, people such as Emile and Airmail, the cross-eyed Cajun twins who played the banjo, and some quiz show host named Rich Dildo, who wore a double-breasted coat that came down to his knees and a bow tie that would spin around like an airplane propeller whenever he pressed the on switch on the battery pack in his pocket.

After a while, the White River Kid and Apple Lisa came up out of the woods, walking slowly and holding hands, and sat down on the porch steps and sat there in silence, while Mrs. Weed sat in the swing, Baker Weed in a rocking chair, and me in one of those metal lawn chairs that always gets bird dropping on it. About nine-thirty, Baker Weed said it was getting too late for him and he was going in to bed and Apple Lisa and the White River Kid also went in and got ready for bed. With Reggie and Morales Pittman gone, I got Reggie's bed and the Kid shared a bed again with Elvis Weed, who had been asleep since about eight-thirty. Apple Lisa had her bed, a cot in the hall, and Mrs. Weed went back into the kitchen again, turned on Elvis

Presley music (I do not know whether she had a record player or if it came from a radio), and began again to dance and sing to it, as a treatment for her cancer. I was very tired and there was a breeze coming in the window by the bed, the dog was asleep on the sofa, sound asleep and snoring, and before long, so was I.

The next morning after breakfast, I took the Kid into the bathroom to put a new bandage on his face and this was the first time I got a chance to see what Doc Poole had done. The place where the tattoo had been was now just a light red area with a good scab on it, thanks, I would guess, to Doc Poole's skill with that wire brush and thanks to the Sugardine, the Doc's special mixture, which he said would make the wound heal fast with no scar, and which appeared to be working. When the bandage was off, the Kid looked at his face in the mirror, the first time he had seen it without the butterfly, the telltale, distinctive sign of identification that had marked him to anyone who had read the newspapers. He rubbed the spot, touched it with his fingertip and I asked him if it was sore and he said no, and right as I watched, his face took on a look that told me he was sorry it was gone, the butterfly that had been there for who knows how many years, a look almost of being terrified and I knew I had to say something to keep him from letting the removal of the butterfly get to him too hard, make him do something crazy, and I said, as softly as I knew how, "Kid, you're safe now. You're safe, no one will know who you are now with the butterfly gone and you will never have to worry about any more deputies hiding in the darkness waiting to gun you down."

I went on like that while I was washing the scar, putting more Sugardine on it, and then rebandaging it, and the Kid calmed down and seemed to adjust to the butterfly being gone and I breathed a little easier. Then I told him it was time to go to work and he asked what work and I told him Baker Weed was going to put him to work in his business, like Apple Lisa had said he would, that he was going to be a salesman in the Weed rabbit hutch and minnow bucket business and the Kid looked a little bewildered then smiled and said did I mean it and I said yes. The Kid said he had never had a job before, that he had never worked anywhere for anyone, and I could tell he was scared about what having a job involved and I reassured him by telling him Apple Lisa's daddy would show him everything he needed to know and so we went out on the front porch in the early morning. It was cool and the grass was still wet with the dew and things smelled good. Baker Weed was already there, with a big cup of coffee in his hand and when he saw the Kid, he smiled and asked him if he was ready to go to work and the Kid said yes and asked Weed what he was supposed to do and Weed nodded to the rabbit hutches and minnow buckets in the front yard, which had been there since shortly after the end of the Korean War and said all the Kid had to do was sit on the porch alongside him and if someone came up and wanted to buy, the Kid would take his money. And so the Kid sat down in the metal lawn chair and began his first day on the job.

I now knew I could leave anytime I wanted to, that I could go back to traveling the backroads of Arkansas and a little of Missouri and Tennessee and Oklahoma and maybe some into Texas and Louisiana, selling socks at a dollar a bunch in small towns, just like I have been doing for years and that it would make no difference to the White River Kid, that he would not try to stop me, and I could go off, a long way from Block Island and maybe never ever get caught up with for what I had been doing with the Kid, for hauling him out of danger, giving him aid and comfort, for being a party to his killing a man, for hiring a doctor, or at least a medical person to remove his tattoo, and worst of all, for having brought him into the home of Baker Weed, who knew nothing about the Kid's past, who was taking him into his business and soon to bless the union of Apple Lisa, his only daughter, in marriage with the Kid, but who was himself now a party to harboring a fugitive from justice and subject to a long term in prison for doing it, if worse came to worst.

Yes, I had brought the Weeds into the clutches of the law by bringing the White River Kid into their house but you must understand I did not know what the Weeds would be like when

I started out, I did not know I would like them, I did not know I would find Baker Weed a man to be friends with, nor Mrs. Weed to be a kind and generous, if somewhat batty, woman. I had put them in a fix but I did not intend to dwell on it, for it does a man no good to wring his hands and become obsessed with things. When the time came to leave, I would just say good-bye to them all and drive away, back to the life of a peddler, that is exactly what I would do when the time came, but it had not come yet and would not, in my estimate, come for at least another two weeks, because I had to stay around to see that the Kid's scar got treated three times a day with Sugardine and I had to stay until all traces of where that butterfly used to be were healed, until that patch of skin looked just like the rest of his face, in case anything unexpected came up, in case some stranger came around and started asking questions about the bandage or the scar and there was no one around to explain about the skin cancer that had been removed.

Besides that, there was another reason I had to stay. The Kid, growing up almost on his own, living along the bank of the White River and having to care for himself, had turned out to be almost as much of a wild boy as anyone was ever likely to find, almost like those boys you read about in those sensational newspapers, stories with headlines like BOY RAISED BY WOLVES, SNARLS, EATS RAW MEAT or BOY RAISED BY OWLS, CATCHES MICE IN THE DARK. The White River Kid was, I would estimate, twenty-two or twenty-three years old and, as a caseworker would put it, had no social skills. He could not tell time, he knew nothing about how many days in a week, how many weeks in a month, he knew nothing about buying things, about getting the most for his money, he knew nothing about governmental units, cities, counties, states, and while he could read and write at about a fourth-grade level, he could never have gone into a box factory and filled out an application for employment, and I have mentioned a box factory because the White River Kid and Apple Lisa, too, already had that hopeless look that you find on the faces of people who work in box factories.

I am not saying the Kid was feebleminded, far from it, although I could not say the same thing for Apple Lisa Weed, whom I had observed many times behaving in ways that could only mean mental retardation. The White River Kid was a different story altogether and if I were put down in the middle of the Ouachita National Forest and told to live off the land I would a thousand times rather have the White River Kid along with me than an honor graduate of Bob Jones University, because the Kid could live off the land, and had done it, off and on, time and again. Granted, the Kid was just plain crazy, or else he would not go around seeing wooly gums in people's eyes, and killing them, then and there, to release some sort of gaseous entity trapped inside them, and granted, it was foolish to believe he would never see another wooly gum in another set of eyes, and granted, only a dreamy fool, only a man as filled with that nonsense that people are capable of change as the most flit-headed social worker ever to come down the pike, could expect him to settle into life at Block Island and become a peaceable and productive citizen, but that is just what I hoped would happen.

I could not abandon the White River Kid, pull out and leave him to the mercies of our society, our culture, to the jaws of the merchants, and bankers, and lawyers and utility companies, and all the other out-and-out swindlers who would prey on him, so I made a vow to stay as long as it took the Kid's face to heal and use that time, maybe two weeks, maybe three, to do what I could to bring him into reality, to equip him to face life, in the event he was not captured or killed by the law, as far as his past social and intellectual deprivation would permit.

Baker Weed and the Kid sat there on the Weeds' front porch all day, waiting for people to come and buy the minnow buckets and rabbit hutches, just as Baker Weed himself had been doing alone for the past thirty or so years, Weed rocking in the chair and the Kid sitting awhile on the steps, then awhile on a tree stump in the front yard, then back to the porch again. I stayed around the house all morning myself, first washing the van on the outside with the Weeds' garden hose, then sweeping it out with the Weeds' broom, which was worn off at an acute angle, then I gathered up all the dirty clothes I could find, the Weeds' and those that I had bought the Kid in the thrift store and mine, too, and took them up the road to a coin-operated laundry in the business district of Block Island and washed and dried them, then folded them and stacked them neatly on the lower bunk in the back of the van. There was still most of the day left, so I walked over to the little grocery store and had a package or two of cinnamon rolls and a quart of chocolate milk, then I bought a couple of sacks of groceries, odds and ends, things I knew Mrs. Weed could use but would not have the money to spare to get, and took them home to the Weed house.

When I got there, it was not yet noon, Baker Weed and the Kid were sitting around, waiting for customers and Elvis Weed was in the front yard, barefooted, holding on to the trunk of a Spaw sapling with one hand and going round and round it, making a circle in the dust. I took the groceries into the house and gave them to Mrs. Weed, who was wearing a clean Elvis Presley costume and dancing to one of his records, something about not having a wooden heart, and I paused to listen to Presley and stayed to listen to his performance of that song all through to the end and there was one thing that impressed me, it was Presley's enunciation. He pronounced all the syllables, every one, clearly and distinctly, it was a near-perfect demonstration of elocution. I put the things that had to go into the refrigerator away, some real butter, a quart of cream for our coffee, a half gallon of black walnut ice cream, for afternoon eating, and a few other things, then I went back out on the porch and asked Baker if he had had any customers. None today, he said, and I sat down on the front steps as Elvis Weed came over and sat down beside me and started fidgeting, I called it, but I guess he thought he was doing an Elvis Presley impression, something I am sure his mother insisted he practice several times a day.

I felt sorry for that boy. Imagine, being named after Elvis Presley and having a mother who wanted to turn you into an exact duplicate of him. It was almost like my own boyhood, when my own mother, who never read anything but *Photoplay* magazine, was always trying to get me to look like the movie idols of her day, now-forgotten actors such as Edmund Lowe—"High-Ho, with Edmund Lowe"—who looked like Douglas Fairbanks, once, even to the extent of her drawing a pencil-thin mustache on me with a burnt match, just to see how much like Edmund Lowe I could be made to look. I looked down at that pitiful little Elvis Weed, a skinny, chinless boy with weak, draining eyes, already rotted teeth, who was always telling people he was going to be "another E'vis" when he grew up, and I imagined how he would look when he was about fifteen and forced to go to school in some green velvet matador costume, forced by his mother to have his hair dyed jet black and waved and lacquered into place until it looked like a spaceman's helmet and it was all I could do to keep from whispering to him to take an ax and bury it in his nutty old mother's neck, right here and now, but I did not, because that would have just caused the poor boy more trouble than it was worth had he done it, and besides, as I have pointed out, Mrs. Weed had redeeming features.

To entertain him as we sat there on the porch that hot August noonday, I did a few simple magic tricks for him, nothing difficult or complex, just the easy ones, the stock illusions, such as putting a golf ball into a Coke bottle, turning ice cubes into billiard balls, pulling live pigeons out of a music box, turning a basketball into a bowl of goldfish, making the garden hose shoot fire, making the dog walk on his hind legs, plucking a few coins out of the air, drawing a string of silks out of a knothole in the Spaw tree, and then I ended the performance by reading an entire deck of playing cards with my eyes closed, and when it was over, I knew that Elvis Weed was baffled, not only Elvis but Baker Weed and the White River Kid, too, whom I realized had probably never seen magic before, indeed, surely, had never seen it and who must have thought I was supernatural, a notion that frightened me when I thought about it, because the Kid could have seen me as another wooly gum, indeed, the Supreme and Exalted Grand Wooly Gum of All, the demon behind all the misery he had seen in people's eyes and had tried to put an end to, and he might have pulled out his pistol and had at me with it, except I had it locked up in the van.

Baker Weed said that was some show, Elvis Weed just sat there, stupefied, on the steps, and the White River Kid asked me how I did it, which put me at ease, because it showed he realized it was a trick, and also was another indication to me that he had a high IQ, or else he would have sat there like Elvis, stunned at what he must have felt was God come down from on high to fool him.

Mrs. Weed came out on the porch drying her hands on a white apron and said "Dinner is ready" and of course, she did not mean "dinner" like you would think of it, getting dressed up and going to Chez Philippe in the Peabody Hotel in Memphis and being shown to a table by a man in a tuxedo and then being attended by other men in tuxedos and one in a tuxedo with a gold chain and some medallion on it hanging around his neck, who made a big thing of helping you select the right wine, and where you were then served a lot of food, all mixed together so that you did not know what any of it was but suspected there was some fish in amongst it, and where you then paid a man one hundred and eighty dollars and were then permitted to leave. No, she meant the noonday meal when she said "dinner," because that was what they called it, these Block Island people, the noonday meal and the meal at five-thirty or six o'clock at night was called "supper." So we went into the house, into the heat, and sat at the table in the kitchen, all of us, me, Baker Weed, Mrs. Weed, Apple Lisa, Elvis Weed, and the White River Kid, and had dinner, fried bologna sandwiches on day-old light bread with mayonnaise and ice tea. After the sandwiches, Mrs. Weed served up little bowls of the ice cream I had brought home, and it must not have been every day that the Weeds had ice cream because Elvis Weed asked his mother what it was.

After dinner, Baker Weed asked us, meaning the men, me and the Kid and Elvis, how we would like it if he closed up the store out front and took us fishing, and Elvis said he would like it, and the Kid got excited, too, and said he wanted to go fishing, yes, he would really like to, so, the upshot of it was that within a half hour of finishing dinner, we were hiking down a road out back of the Weed house, carrying fishing poles and tackle boxes, headed to the cutoff, a place Baker Weed said was two miles away, and which we could only reach by walking because there was no real road and any vehicle would risk getting stuck in mud up to the tops of the tires, anyway.

We were not a hundred yards from the house before I wished I had not come, for we were by then deep into what was surely a snake-infested area, close, overhanging growth, marshy ground, no path to speak of, and I did not have on the proper shoes for such an outing, no cowhide work shoes, or army boots, just a pair of white leather low quarters, or what a lot of people in Arkansas would call "slippers." Baker Weed kept on, beating a path, followed by Elvis, who also knew the way, then me and the Kid bringing up the rear. Here and there beside the path was a pool of stagnant water, and once or twice I saw things slithering through them, going under logs, and every now and then, a turtle would jump off a log and splash into the water and the sound would give me a scare, and I would say to myself, if I get back home from this trip without having some snake sink his fangs in the meat of my ass, I would thank the Fates in some proper and impressive way and never let myself get into such a fix again.

Baker Weed kept on, sometimes leading us across pools of water that came up over my shoe tops, always heading deeper into the underbrush to the cutoff, walking fast, Elvis keeping up. Once in a while I turned to see how the Kid was making it, and he would smile when he saw me and I realized this Arkansas wilderness was his home territory, he had no fear, this sort of place was where he had spent his boyhood but I had no time to talk to him because Baker Weed was pressing on and calling back to us, asking if we "was played out" and could we keep up, and to come on, there was just about another half mile to go. I was getting snagged on thorns, and the mosquitoes were so thick I was breathing them into my nostrils and I was miserable, but I kept on going, because it somehow made me think of those daylong hikes we had to take in the army and I remembered the times then when I almost gave up, when I wanted to just throw down my pack and fall asleep alongside the trail but I did not, because to do so would have let down my outfit, embarrassed my buddies and made me feel ashamed later and so I kept on then, and I kept on now, knowing how much pride I would take in having made the effort when it was all over.

We finally got to a place where the path consisted of nothing but little mounds of dirt sticking out of the water and we had to jump from one to the other which was not easy when one weighed as much as I do and when one was also carrying a fishing pole but at least there was less brush growing over our heads and I did not feel as if I was being swallowed by branches and shrubbery, all of it with long thorns. I was getting ready to jump to the next mound, getting up a head of steam, as it were, when the Kid touched my shoulder and I turned to see what he wanted and he had his finger up to his lips in a sign to be still, be quiet, then he pointed down to the ground, not three feet from where I stood, to a snake stretched out full-length on the ground, a long black snake, one of those with the triangular-shaped head which meant viper, fangs that spilled venom. I just had a second to take in the snake, to let it register on my brain, no time to think of what to do, develop a plan of behavior to deal with it, for the Kid moved in, quicker than lightning, stooped down and grabbed that snake by its tail then drew it back over his shoulder and cracked it like a whip. There was a noise like a pistol shot and I saw the snake's head flying off in the air to my right and then the Kid threw the snake's dead body into the water and he laughed, laughed like I had not seen him laugh since I had known him, the laughter of happiness, of being at home again.

I had witnessed something I had heard tell of but had never seen, the snapping off of a snake's head from the force of the whip crack on its body, and I am now prepared to say it can be done, that it is not just a bit of folklore, for I had actually seen the White River Kid pick up a snake at least six feet long and kill it in an instant, no struggle, on the first try. The Kid laughed some more and I said to him, what kind of a snake was that, it looked poisonous to me, and he said it was just an old moccasin and they cannot hurt you unless they bite you. Baker Weed had turned to see how we were coming about the time the Kid had drawn the snake back over his head and I could tell he was impressed with his soon to be son-in-law for he said to the Kid, you sure handled that one smooth and said if it had been him, he would have just tried to push it out of the way with his fishing pole.

Here we are, said Baker Weed, this is the cutoff and he pointed to a lake about the size of five or six football fields, laid side to side, lengthways. The water was dark, maybe a gray, maybe more of a deep green, and there was tangled underbrush growing right down to the water's edge all around it. It had a primeval look to me, like one of those places no white man has ever seen before, maybe only a few Indians, where alligators and gar and catfish and turtles and snakes of all kinds had lived, feeding off each other, for eons. I was afraid to set my foot down after the experience with that snake, and afraid to sit down anywhere, knowing another moccasin would crawl up from under something and go for me, for it is common knowledge that a moccasin will do just that, attack a man who has startled it, whereas most other snakes will move away when somebody comes up on them.

I happened to look down at the ground and I saw a bunch of tiny baby snakes, I do not know what kind, squirming along in the mud and I knew this was no place for Brother Edgar of the Little Brothers of St. Mortimer, who was well known for being much more at home sitting down to the house special plate lunch in the principal cafe of some lively town of about six thousand than he is for getting down on all fours in a reptile garden. Baker Weed and Elvis Weed did not seem to be afraid of anything that might turn up alongside that lake and they started wading out into it, baiting hooks and getting ready to fish.

Wading into the murk? I would not have felt safe wading into such a body of water unless I was wearing a new pair of Cats

Foot Waders, an item of waterproof footware sold in those specialty catalogs, made of vulcanized rubber and having ripple tread on the bottom to prevent slipping on slimy rocks, but there was no such item available and I decided I would try to find a safe place to sit or otherwise wait until the others had had enough and wanted to head back home.

The White River Kid, on the other hand, looked like a child who had been invited to a picnic in a candy store, he looked as excited as de Soto must have looked when he first saw the Mississippi River on that bluff at Memphis. The Kid let out a yell, something like "Yiphee!" and started taking off his clothes, pulling off his shoes first, then his shirt, pants, and underwear, then he waded into the water and when he was out deep enough he started splashing around like a young seal, diving under, swimming underwater awhile, then coming up, splashing, shaking the water out of his eyes and his hair, then laughing and going back under again.

I yelled to him, "Kid, come out of that filthy water, you'll get that place on your face infected!" but he was not listening, he just kept on swimming, diving, staying under, then surfacing, obviously having the time of his life. Baker Weed was getting impatient, because the Kid's splashing in the water made it impossible for him to fish and he yelled to the Kid, "Hey, young fella, come on out of that water so we can catch a few catfish for supper" and when the Kid heard the word *catfish* he said to Baker Weed, "You just hold up and I'll get you a catfish."

He dived back into the water again and this time he stayed down in that murky lake for a long time, so long it scared me, it was nearly three minutes, I would guess and I was getting ready to try and do something to get him back up out of there, although I had no idea what I could do since I had no boat and was not a good swimmer myself and I knew Baker Weed and Elvis Weed could do nothing either, when the Kid broke water and he was dragging something big that was fighting him in a frenzy.

The Kid swam up to the shore then to the part where he could stand up in the water and started pulling that thing up after him. It was a catfish, maybe the biggest catfish I had ever seen, I would guess about sixty pounds and the Kid said to Baker Weed, "Here's you a catfish," and I then realized how he got it and knew that I was witnessing the second thing I had thought might be folklore in the same afternoon, I had seen a man stump fishing, which is what they call the technique the White River Kid used to catch that catfish.

Stump fishing, it is illegal and sometimes dangerous, but it is based on the knowledge that there are always great large catfish at the very bottom of lakes like this one, huge fish that stay on the bottom, sometimes inside old hollow stumps and they are so placid that a good swimmer can go down there to the bottom where they are and if he can see one inside a stump, he can put his hand in there and actually stroke the fish, and they will not move or attack, and the experienced stump fisherman will keep on stroking that old catfish until he can get his hands inside its mouth and lock on and then it is just a matter of getting the fish to the top, pulling him right on out of that stump then getting him to the bank, which is just what the White River Kid had done. When he presented this enormous fish to Baker Weed, Weed was as pleased in his new son-in-law as a man can be, and it also meant that now they had enough catfish for supper, they did not need to stay there at the cutoff any longer, for Baker Weed had not gone fishing for sport or for relaxation, or for the thrill of fighting a game fish. He went to catch food for supper and now that he had it, only a fool would stay around.

The Kid took one end and Elvis the other and they started carrying the fish back to the house. We got back in about an hour going the same way we had come, jumping from one mound to another but we saw no more snakes and the trip was uneventful.

When we got home, I was as tired as I had been in years, almost too tired to take a bath, but I had to, to wash the scratches on my arms and neck, and just to try and wash off the memory of that gloomy tarn, and that journey to the center of the earth. The best part about doing something that makes you very tired, something like heavy labor, or a long hike, is the deep relaxed sleep that you can have if you are free to go to bed right then and there. I was free to and I went to my room and passed out on the bed after my bath, and had a deep, dreamless sleep.

The Kid and Elvis stayed out in the yard, cleaning and skinning the catfish, and Baker Weed went back to work at his retail outlet, sitting on the porch, dozing off and on while waiting for customers.

I was awakened by Elvis at about six o'clock and the first thing I smelled was fried fish and I knew Mrs. Weed had fried that catfish. I went into the kitchen where she had set the table for supper and all the others were already there, waiting for me, and as soon as I sat down, they started passing the food, fried catfish steaks, fried potatoes, Bermuda onions, sliced and served in a bowl of cold vinegar, hot peppers, corn bread, and Royal instant chocolate pudding for dessert, and I ate and ate, maybe three pieces of that fish, and had lots of butter on my corn bread and a little Louisiana hot sauce, and we all ate our fill, and everyone was happy, and the Kid and Apple Lisa were sitting next to each other and rubbing their legs and it was a wonderful family evening and I enjoyed it all I could, closing my mind to the truth, that the White River Kid was a killer and that these good people, maybe even me, might be in danger from him.

After supper, Baker Weed and I went out on the porch with a fresh glass of ice tea and sat there, sipping our tea and watching the sun go down.

TEN

The next ten days were as near to a vacation as I had ever had. The weather turned cool, even nippy, as it will sometimes do in these parts in August, and I was able to sleep comfortably every night, never once waking up bathed in sweat and my mouth dry, and what with the money I gave her for groceries, and the fact that I went in to the little grocery store in town where the Weeds had a long overdue bill for groceries they had bought on credit, a one-man operation, a small concrete and brick building with a spongy wood floor and smelling of kerosene and fly spray, and paid the bill up to date in full, thus enabling the Weeds to charge more groceries, Mrs. Weed fixed some elegant meals for me, such as sauerkraut and backbones; meat loaf with two strips of bacon on top; fried chicken and mashed potatoes; hot cakes and sausage; cheese grits and meat patties and fried okra; fried corn, cut right off the cob; and desserts every meal, usually Royal instant pudding, but sometimes cold rice with sugar, vanilla, and milk on it.

I had planned to spend the time it took for the Kid's scar to heal trying to teach him things he would need to know. In fact, at first I was going to let him in on a little secret I have had for years, the knowledge of a technique that has helped me through many a financial tight spot, namely a substance which I call Brother Edgar's Special Document Spray. When I was no more than thirteen or so, my father gave me a chemistry set for Christmas and while it in itself was of no long-range use to me, for all I learned to do with it was to make blue ink and to do a magic trick that involved a lot of empty jars and a pitcher of tap water and I would pour the water into the empty jars and it would look like I was pouring different colored liquids out of the same pitcher, still the chemistry set helped me.

It got me interested in mixing up things, pouring one liquid into another, common household items, mostly, and seeing what would happen. I nearly died when I poured laundry bleach into ammonia and the fumes it created got into my lungs, but I did have one lucky accident, serendipity, you might call it. I had mixed up three liquids, one of them was rubbing alcohol and I am not going to tell you the other two, because I need to hold on to something of value as I am getting older, and had produced a colorless and nearly odorless liquid that seemed to have no interesting characteristics and while I cannot now recall exactly how it happened, I chanced to spray a little of this liquid on some paper, an accident, it was, like most important discoveries, saccharin being one that comes to mind, and I did not even realize I had sprayed the piece of paper and had no idea of what was going to happen, but something did, and I happened, also by accident, to be watching the paper as it just disappeared in front of my eyes, gone into nothingness, not even any dust or crumbs.

I was young and knew little of chemistry, but I had enough experience to realize I had hit upon something of great importance. I took a fresh piece of paper, tough, heavy stationery, and sprayed it with the liquid. In ten minutes, the paper was gone, leaving not a trace and no odor or other hint of its ever having been in existence. For the next few days, I conducted experiments with this magic liquid I had created out of common household items and each time, the paper I sprayed vanished, and what is more important, it was not necessary to soak the paper in the liquid to get it to dissolve, for all you had to do was spray it just slightly, an even coat that dried as soon as it was applied.

As I have been telling you all along in this narrative, and hope I have now established by giving examples and making revelations, I have never been what you could call comfortable with the rules of society, especially the society in the Tri-Cities area of East Texas, where I grew up, which held that it was a boy's duty to work hard so that others could prosper, and be content with the pension you got, a pension, in my youth, never being over forty-three dollars a month and sometimes, including a free pass on the railroad. So, as soon as I realized I had a valuable property in this liquid I had concocted, I started trying to think of ways to use it to enrich myself and I will be frank and state I did not have enough sense to just get a patent on it and license some chemical company to manufacture it and sell it and pay me a small royalty off each bottle sold. I may yet do that, but when I first discovered it, the only thing that occurred to me to do with it was to find a way to cheat the upper class, and it was not long before I thought of banks and bankers, it having been my experience up to that time, and since confirmed by nearly forty more years of close observation, that there is no group in our society more deserving of a little of their own medicine, that is, being done out of their money, than banks, and although I was not able to put it into effect at once, since it involved opening a checking account and I was not considered of a proper age until I was about twenty-two, but once I had a checking account I started in with my plan and have been doing it ever since.

Simply put, this is how I have worked it. I opened a checking account at the Tenant Farmers Bank and Trust Company in North Little Rock, Arkansas, J. Tiberius Meal, Vice President and Cashier, as soon as I was old enough for such an account to look legitimate, and I made deposits and wrote checks on it for a year, always taking great care to maintain it in good standing.

Then, after all the tellers knew me, and never paid any attention to me when I came and went, I went into the bank and presented one of my checks, drawn in the amount of five dollars, payable to cash, to the teller, who, knowing me as a good and reliable customer, cashed it in an instant and put it away in the drawer with all the other checks she had cashed that day. Before entering the bank, in fact, while in my automobile in the bank parking lot, I sprayed that check with my solution, waved it in the air a time or two to be sure it was dry, and presented it, knowing it would dissolve in the teller's drawer and that there would be no evidence of my transaction to justify the bank deducting five dollars from the balance in my checking account. When the statement arrived from the bank at the end of the month, I opened it and looked to see if the five dollars had been deducted and it had not, assuring me that the check had in fact dissolved in the drawer before the teller had closed out the total for that day, leaving her five dollars short when all the books were balanced. I went slow at first, cashing one or two treated checks a month, always in round figures, usually ten dollars, and time went by, the years passed, and I was never charged for any of the checks I cashed, and it got to where I was cashing big checks, usually one hundred dollars, only on busy days, however, when I knew there would be lots of transactions and on those days, I would make a point of coming in to the same teller twice on the same day, generally to make a deposit and later to cash a check, or sometimes, making a deposit and cashing a check at the same time. I had no idea how the bank was handling this until years later when I got to know Tiberius Meal, himself, who, thinking me a Brother, once sat down beside me in the White Eagle Cafe and started to confide in me, to the effect that he had had to fire another teller, this must be about the twelfth he had fired, because of stealing, because of their drawer coming up short, usually a hundred dollars, every now and then.

I sympathized with Meal and tired to console him by telling him that in my line, a traveling Brother, I saw the underside of society and he had no idea the extent to which people were tempted by money. He sort of sobbed a little, and set down his coffee cup, and whispered the information that his tellers were stealing from him with such regularity and by means no accountant could detect, to the extent that the bonding companies would no longer cover his help and he was at this moment operating a full service bank with no surety bonds on them. One really big theft out of those cash drawers would wipe him out, he said, and while he could prosecute the tellers, it would not bring back the money and I took old man Meal's hand and actually patted the back of it and told him I would pray to the Lord to ask that such a thing not come to pass.

So, I had thought about letting the Kid in on the secret of how to make money from your checking account and actually sat him down the first day or so of my planned schooling and tried to explain to him about banks themselves, to start with, and then about checks and I was trying my best to get the concepts across when I realized the Kid was just too inexperienced to be able to handle the whole notion and I gave up, and not without some sadness because you will have picked up by now that I had come to think of the Kid as a son. I sort of had the idea that giving the Kid my secret formula and turning him loose on the banks would be like passing on an inheritance, that I would leave him something, but I finally had to admit to myself that the Kid was just not equipped to handle anything as sophisticated as Brother Edgar's Document Spray and I forgot about it, as far as letting the Kid in on it was concerned and I decided to try to teach him other things, such as society's rules and expectations and how to do things and who and what to watch out for and the importance of learning to be places on time and to stay for regular periods of time.

I asked the Kid if he would like to go to school and he said yes and asked where, and I told him I was a school teacher and I would set up a school right there at the house and teach him things he needed to know and this surprised the Kid, who had attended school, maybe up as far as the sixth grade, while living with his mother and in foster homes and he had never seen or heard of or ever thought of a man as a school teacher, and I had to explain to him that there were many men who were school teachers and the Kid accepted that but said he had never liked school and had run away from it as often as he could, but when I told him the school would be here at the Weed house and would only last two hours a day, for two hours is as long as I thought I could keep the Kid's mind on it, he said it sounded all right and so I told him we would start the next morning.

I ran a school for the Kid about five days and then it just played out. I started the next morning after I had taken the bandage off his face and washed the place where the tattoo had been with Sugardine and put a fresh bandage on it. We went out in the front yard, under the Spaw tree, and sat on boxes and at first I tried to improve his reading and writing, which, as I have said, were at about a fourth grade level, or roughly the equivalent of the typical big city high school graduate, but not really adequate to get by in the world. I tried to explain phonics to him, that each letter of the alphabet represented, or was a symbol for a sound that could be made by the human voice, but I got nowhere, for the Kid's short time in school had been spent under teachers with graduate hours in education, who had abandoned phonics as old fashioned, and who were trying to teach reading by having students learn to recognize whole words and the Kid just found it all too confusing. I tried to improve his handwriting, but he did not have the patience to practice penmanship, and when I realized he could not tell time, did not know the order of the days in the week, and had no desire to learn, I gave up on formal education and tried things like giving him a new identity. He did not know his birthday, his father's name, he knew only that his mother's name was Bitsie, so I tried to invent a past for him, I tried to get him to grasp that his name was W. R. Bird, no name, just initials, and that he was born at Berryville, Arkansas; father's name, W. R. Bird; mother's name, Bitsie Smith Bird.

It was all beyond him and I realized I was dealing with a young man who was almost a total blank, who knew nothing much beyond how to fuck and how to load a pistol and how to pull the trigger, and I gave up, as I have said, after five days, just quit trying to help him. I rationalized it by telling myself he did not have long to go, anyway, not much time left before he went back to seeing wooly gums in people's eyes, and was brought down by some peace officer's gun. I told myself that day might be just over the next sunrise and if I was smart, I would be long gone and far away when it happened and as I have said, I was staying around just long enough for that scar on the Kid's face to heal completely and with the three daily applications of Doc Poole's Sugardine, it was doing very well and I started letting the Kid go without a bandage after the third day, and after a week, there was no question it was going to heal completely and leave no trace of the tattoo or its removal.

Reluctantly, but realizing there was nothing else I could do, I told the Kid he could quit school again, that he already knew all he needed to know, anyway, and he smiled and appeared to agree with me. I closed down the school, added schoolmaster to the list of professions I had followed, and from then on every morning after breakfast, the Kid and Apple Lisa would go off together into those gloomy woods and swamps near the house and stay all day, the Kid not even paying any attention to the job he was supposed to have as a salesman for Baker Weed's minnow buckets and rabbit hutches. And so, for the rest of the time I stayed visiting the Weeds, I would sit on the porch alongside Baker Weed, in the cool of the morning, under the shade of the Spaw tree and we would talk about the things old men from Arkansas had in common.

The first thing I asked Baker Weed was what he knew or could remember about the big explosion called the Block Island Catastrophe that had created the huge crater at one end of town and what it was they made in the factory. His father and his grandfather and Mrs. Weed's father and two uncles, all men who had never before had jobs because there was just no work in the area, had been hired on at the factory when it first opened, he said, and they worked unloading trucks filled with bauxite, the ore from which aluminum is made, all day and all night, until there was a mound of bauxite as tall as a mountain and covering as much area, and still they kept bringing in trucks loaded with bauxite, all of it from the bauxite mines near Little Rock. The factory was built to make a special kind of aluminum, said Baker Weed, stronger and lighter than regular aluminum, and they were going to make it at Block Island because of the Spitticinnia granules found in great quantity in the Block Island area, found there then, back in the forties, and still there today, anywhere you turned up a shovelful of earth.

Baker Weed's father got to work inside the factory after a while, shoveling the Spitticinnia granules onto a conveyor belt that fed into a furnace where the bauxite ore and the Spitticinnia were fused and united by the fire. The notion of mixing bauxite and Spitticinnia to produce an extra-lightweight and stronger aluminum was the idea of a scientist from Europe who came to Block Island to live and direct the operation, said Baker Weed, and at first it looked like it was going to work, the mixture of bauxite and Spitticinnia granules, because the first few sheets of aluminum the factory turned out were so light a child could hold up a piece of it as big as a house and it was strong, fearsome strong, said Baker Weed and the whole county was happy about the factory because it looked like it would expand and be there after the war, giving everybody who wanted one a job, and there was no danger of them moving the factory anywhere else because, according to some geologists, the Block Island area was the only place in the world where Spitticinnia granules were to be found and it looked to everyone like the streets of Block Island would soon be paved in gold, but then the bottom fell out of everything.

The scientists discovered that the new aluminum was not stable, they started having problems with it just suddenly bursting into flame and going up in a wisp of green smoke and then one morning, when the factory was filled with men from the area who worked there, and the mountain of bauxite ore was even bigger and there was a mountain of Spitticinnia granules right beside it, there was some kind of reaction, a few sparks were passed from one mountain of ore to another and there was a tremendous explosion, the factory building and all the men inside it disappeared, blown into the heavens, never a body was ever found and the mountains of ore just burned up, clouds of green flame choked the skies of Block Island for days and when all the fires were out and all the dust settled, most of the men in town were gone, presumed dead, vaporized, and the big crater was there, smoke curling out of it all along its sides. After a few years, Baker Weed's mother and the other widows in town got some sort of settlement from the owners of the factory, some pension or another that was just enough to keep body and soul together.

Baker talked a long time about Block Island in the days after the factory opened and before it blew up and about the optimism that everyone had. They opened a movie theatre, the Snag Cinema, on Main Street, and somebody came in from Texarkana and opened up a cafeteria, and a radio preacher came to town and started claiming God had called him to reach out and touch people in a special way and everybody in town had a "Belched Oak" bedroom suite from a new furniture store then opened on Main Street and some fellow started building a high-class housing development that advertised it was going to be near enough to the Moose Club to walk over and play bingo and somebody came into town and started a newspaper called the *Morning Rooster*. It was a great time, full of promise, said Baker Weed, and then it all fell through, all folded, all went back to nothing, when the factory exploded.

Instead of wealth and comfort, all there was left were a lot of widows and orphans and all that optimism had turned into nothing, and when Baker Weed mentioned optimism, I recalled how optimistic I had been at the end of World War II, although I was just fourteen, I was adult enough to know there was going to be a great happy world after the war, with all the bad nations beaten and made over into democracies, and all the benefits of science undertaken in behalf of the war effort now free to be applied to making life better and there was going to be prosperity and comfort and plastics of all kinds that could be sawed, sanded, and nailed just like wood.

Baker Weed got drafted about the same time I did and we

both were sent to Korea and we had lots of memories of it to share and of army duty. We both, for instance, had actually seen General Maxwell Taylor, and both of us came away from the experience with good feelings about him, and we remembered bathing in the rivers and sleeping near the gravesites and the smell of dead men that filled the air, and Baker had actually been in combat, had actually had his unit overrun by the Chinese one night, and remembered being awakened by the cries of his buddies who were dying, bayoneted through their sleeping bags and he said he would always carry the memory of the fellow in his unit who thought combat would be like a movie and when it actually got started one day, when Baker's unit was ordered to take a hill and they spread out in a line and started walking up it slowly, each man firing a round to some kind of internal metronome, and the Chinese started fighting back, started throwing down mortar rounds from the top of that hill and all hell was breaking loose and this young soldier was bewildered and started screaming, "Where's the music? Where's the music?" like he expected some sort of background music to life itself.

I had to worm it out of Baker Weed, sitting there in a pair of overalls, barefooted, the fact that he was decorated for gallantry in action two times during the war, and that he killed a few Chinamen while doing it, sometimes with rifle bullets but sometimes with knives and sometimes with hand grenades. I had to pull the facts out of him because he did not like to recall it, and I am probably to be criticized for making him do it, but he sort of brought up the subject himself when he started talking about the schooling he got after the war. When he came back to Block Island, he had the GI Bill that would pay for his education and as he put it, he "had the notion to make a preacher" and he enrolled in something called The Dark of Night Bible College in Whiff, Texas, about ten miles from Block Island. The first thing they told him there was that the Lord had said "Thou shall not kill" and yet here was his government, hauling him across the country, then across the Pacific Ocean and setting him down in a foreign land, where he did not know a single native of the place, and equipping him and setting him to kill, to kill as many as he could and after a week in The Dark of Night Bible College, he realized life is full of conflicts and there was nothing a man could do about it, so he dropped out of college and went back to Block Island and opened his minnow bucket and rabbit hutch business.

I would spend the mornings talking to Baker Weed and then I would walk up the street into town and get me a bottle of chocolate milk and a honey bun at the gas station and before long, I was a friend of the man who owned it, a fat fellow named Travis who was getting bald, and it was not long before I put the question to him, whereabouts in this town can a man find a little action. And Travis, while he may have spent his life keeping store in the backwaters of civilization, knew exactly what I was talking about and he said there was none that he knew of in town, unless it might be Eva Nell LaFangroy, whom he described as kind of a "wild lady" who lived about three blocks from the Weeds' house, on the road leading to the woods, and who I could find easy enough because she always had a yard sale going on at her house.

I asked Travis if he had ever been with Eva Nell LaFangroy and he shook his head and said, "I ain't scroon so much as a Portuguese man-of-war since last Christmas," in a tone that could have meant he was sanctified and refused to defile the temple of his body, or that he had just had no luck, and I did not press the point but made a mental note to look up Miss Eva Nell LaFangroy as soon as the opportunity presented itself.

That night, I was dressing the Kid's face with Sugardine and observing that I hardly need to do even that anymore because it was healing so nicely and while swabbing his cheek, I asked him what it was he and Apple Lisa did all day long in those woods and he answered in sort of a monotone, "We fuck," and I asked then what and he said, "We fuck some more," and then what, I asked, and he said then they lay on their backs and looked up into the treetops and Apple Lisa said she could always see little birds up there, birds you could see through, little sweet birds that never lit on anything and the Kid said he could not see the birds and he said that at night, when they were alone in the woods, they would lie on their backs and look up at the sky and try to see shooting stars. The Kid said Apple Lisa told him she had never seen a shooting star, never in her life and did not know what one was and they lay there sometimes for hours in the dark, looking for shooting stars, because that was one thing the Kid wanted to show Apple Lisa, a shooting star, but they never saw one.

The next morning, after my visit on the porch with Baker Weed, I started walking along the road to the woods, looking for the home of Eva Nell LaFangroy and before long, I saw a sign nailed to a tree that said Yard Sale Today and had an arrow on it pointing the way ahead. I turned a curve in the road and saw her, sitting on the ground in her front yard next to a wooden apple box set on one end, with a broken-down-looking pop-up toaster on it. When I got near to her, she ran a hand through her hair and asked me, "Do you need any appliances?" and pointed to the toaster. I sort of hemmed and hawed, and did not commit myself, hoping to get her to talking so I could "read" her, see what she was like and as is usual with me, it was not long before I had not only read her, but we were talking about screwing, her and me, and I asked her if she had a husband and she said no, no husband, no income, just a poor girl on her own.

A good-looking poor girl, I thought to myself, for in fact, Miss Eva Nell LaFangroy was one of the best-looking women I had ever run into socially in my life, being about thirty-five, well built, big tits, a round little ass, good-looking skin, perfect teeth, all any man could ask for and she was vibrant, too, full of life, given to laughing, so bright I am sure she would have glowed in the dark.

I could not understand why she was stuck here in Block Island when she could have been making a pot of money as a hooker in any hotel in Little Rock. Several possibilities crossed my mind, first of which was the probability that she was an alcoholic. I tried to keep her talking to see what I could conclude about her and I asked if she had a boyfriend and she said not anymore, that he had left and I asked where he went and why he left and she said he left because he got bit by a tree frog, right there in her living room and she turned and pointed to the house, and I started to conclude that she must be a little off in the head, and I concluded that definitely when she said she did not know where he was but he might have been eaten by a neighboring wolf. She said she did not care if he was gone because he thought sex was dirty. It is dirty, she said to me, but not enough, and let out a good healthy laugh. I asked her to tell me more about her boyfriend, who she said was a musician who did birds on a flute for radio commercials, but who had lots of hang-ups. I asked her to tell me about his hang-ups and she said the first time they ever talked about screwing she asked him if there was anything kinky he liked to do and he hung his head and confessed there was, and she said what is it, and he said it was too awful, that she would not want to have anything to do with him if he told her, and she hung on, and finally insisted he tell her what it was he liked to do that was so kinky it would repel her and finally, he hung his head and said that he liked to "get nekkid when I do it." "Can you imagine that?" she asked me, "a man so hung up he thinks it was dirty to get naked?" I told her I did find that hard to imagine and I asked her what she had done when he told her that and she said she had made him take off his clothes and had whipped his ass with a peach tree switch until it bled and then had left him tied to a tree in the backyard all night as a means of helping him get rid of his inhibitions.

If you have been a close reader of this narrative so far, you will recall my casual mention of fondness for having a woman whip my ass with a length of fan belt from a cotton gin, and when Miss LaFangroy told me what she had done to her boy-friend, I almost experienced stoppage of the heart from the excitement of finding a woman like her, here in this near-aban-doned backwater. Of course, I did not let her know that I was having a racing heart at the notion of getting whipped, because if she had any sophistication at all, she would know she could get her price out of me, even if it was the moon, so all I said was, "whipped him with a switch, did you? I have heard of men who like that sort of thing, yes, sometimes, I have even thought, myself, it might be an exciting thing to experience." Well, in no time, we had agreed on a price, I was to pay her twenty dollars, in exchange for which I would get the toaster, which looked like a fire hazard to me, and she would drive off into the woods with me in the van, which I hurried back to the Weeds' house to get. Soon, she was sitting beside me, in the seat opposite the driver, and directing me along the road, deep into the woods, in the direction of Socrates. She explained we could not use her house because her old father was asleep inside it, and would probably be awakened by the sound of "a whip cutting at your ass" as she put it. She kept on giving me directions until we came to a side road, which I was afraid I could not get the van along but she said it would be possible because only last week, she had brought a truck driver into this area, in his tractor and trailer rig, and he had no trouble getting out. We arrived at a spot and she said to get out, go over to that tree trunk, drop my pants and get ready, and I handed her the piece of fan belt and ran over as fast as one my age and weight could do, to do exactly as she ordered, for this looked like it was going to be about as much fun, if not more, than what I heretofore recalled as the most thrilling time I have ever had, an afternoon ten or so years ago, when a Mrs. Key of Key Largo, Florida, kept me bent over a Spanish cannon for about two hours on the beach while she gave me a work-over with a whip made of plaited sharkskin. I dropped my pants and bent over the tree trunk and waited for the first cut of the fan belt and it was great, well placed and well delivered and Miss LaFangroy kept on applying it and I was just about to get off the biggest load of all time, for I am one of those lucky ones who can reach a climax just by being whipped and I do not have to manipulate anything at all, when she stopped and started screaming, "Run! Run! Back to the truck! Hurry!" and I grog-gily came back to reality and said, "What? What are you talking about?" and she screamed again, "Run!" and started pulling my pants back up for me and trying to get me back to the van. I still did not know what was going on when she pointed to the woods about twenty yards away, and I saw a cloud of dust and saw the bushes shaking and the whole area seemed to be rumbling and I thought it was an earthquake until she said, "It's a mess of wild hogs! Hurry! They'll eat us alive!" and she started running for the van. By this time, I had returned to reality and realized what she was talking about and also hurried as fast as I could back to the safety of the van and we both got inside it and slammed the door just as one ugly old hog with long razor-sharp tusks made a dash for us and plowed right smack into the side of the van, almost turning it over, or so it seemed. From inside the van, we could see thirty or more wild hogs rooting in a frenzy where we had been, then standing up on their back legs, trying to see in the van, and bumping it and snorting and chewing at the tires. We were prisoners, I could not back up, I could not go forward. I tried to scare them by starting the engine and gunning it and honking the horn but they would not go away. We stayed in the van a half hour, her trying to earn the money I had paid her, trying to get me off, first with the fan belt, but there was no room in the van to get a good backswing, then by hand, and finally she went down on it and I got it off while the hogs were thumping against the side of the van, trying to open the metal can, as it were, to get inside at us and eat us alive. After a time, maybe another hour, all the hogs had gone on to other mischief, and I was able to back out of those woods and get Miss LaFangroy back to her house. I was infuriated at those hogs that had ruined my little stolen moment with Miss LaFangroy and I knew it would never be the same thrill it had started out to be, but then I remembered what a good turn the hogs had done to me, eating up the Bunn brothers to the absolute tiniest part and I could not bring myself to hold a grudge against them, and accepted the order of things, a nature where everything has its place.

ELEVEN

had been stopping at the Weeds' nearly ten days and I
was getting restless, for there was nothing to do at
their house, there was nothing to read, no music to
listen to, no soft white pine chunks to carve into farm animals,
and I had been back once to see Miss Eva Nell LaFangroy and
even that, while still almost enough thrill to kill me outright,
had grown old. I guess I was restless, or just bored, staying in
one house for that long, me, a man who had been on the road
selling socks for years, never staying in any one town over two
days, and it occurred to me that I could break up the monotony
of waiting for that scar on the Kid's face to totally heal, to
disappear altogether, by driving the van to some town nearby
and setting up shop in the square, like I had been doing before I
met the Kid, setting up the card table and selling some socks
and maybe collecting a few dollars in the HELP US PAY FOR EYE
SURGERY jug. Maybe I could even get some more entries in the
Poetry Contest, so come Saturday morning, that is just what I
did, I drove from Block Island over to the county seat, a town
of about five thousand, called Peasley Grove, and I had Apple

Lisa and the White River Kid with me and, here, I will have to state that there was really no longer any reason for me to stay around him and the Weed family and the town of Block Island, for his face was entirely healed, by that I mean, you could not tell he had ever had a butterfly tattooed on his left cheek and there was no sign whatever of it having been sandpapered off, for his face looked as normal as any that had never been tampered with.

While I had been telling myself these past ten days that I had to stay around to keep the Kid from being recognized, now that there was no longer any danger of it, I could not bring myself to leave and since I am a man who prides himself on being able to read people, to account from close observation for why they behave as they do, I felt I had to read myself and see what it was that was making me stay around these people, this cold-blooded, crazy killer, the White River Kid, and his daffy, mean-spirited girlfriend Apple Lisa, and her old mother and daddy and that sorrowful little Elvis Weed. I admitted to myself that, as inadequate as they all were, as far from the optimum as they might be, those people had become my family, the only family I had ever really had, and when one gets as old as I am, when the gates of that county nursing home are yawning—where moronic farm women come to the city to seek their fortune, and who will find it in employment as nursing attendants, will talk baby talk to me and put me aside in paper diapers—he holds on to family, even a family as hard to explain as this one was, so there I was, transporting the White River Kid and Apple Lisa back along a highway to set up as a peddler in a town square.

I got to Peasley Grove early on Saturday morning and got set up, as usual, the card table out, the socks stacked high on it, the donation jug set out in a prominent place and I put on some of my Brother's regalia, the chain and cross around my neck, the belt of knotted rope around my waist, and I was back in business and off to a good start, even welcomed and given a waved greeting by a policeman who passed in a squad car, slowed down, smiled and said, "Good morning, Father" to me.

It looked like it would be a good day, the town started filling up with farmers and people who lived off the unpaved roads, in town to shop, and by nine-thirty, I had sold maybe thirty bundles of socks, seen at least five dollars in small change dropped into the eye surgery jug and had accepted a few poems from a young man who said he was going away to school to get a degree in agriculture and who intended to major in poultry vaccines, and try to do a little extra work in the fields of figs and bananas.

All this time, the White River Kid and Apple Lisa had sat right there on a curb, near the truck, behaving like a young lady and young gentleman should, and more than once I even introduced them to sock buyers as "some of our young people," but by ten o'clock, both were getting fidgety and fretful and it occurred to me that it would do no harm to give them a little folding money and turn them loose in town, let them play married couple and do a little shopping, go in a few stores. I knew it would probably be safe enough because the Kid had no identifying scar on his face and he did not have the gun, which I had locked in a chest under one of the bunks and I even looked into the van, sort of casually, so as the Kid would not get the idea I was spying on him, and saw that the chest was still padlocked, so I asked the two of them if they would like to walk around the square and maybe get a hamburger and do a little shopping. To make it possible, I gave each one ten dollars, and the Kid took his and looked at it for the longest time and I realized he was overwhelmed, that he had never in his life had that much money before. I told him and Apple Lisa to be careful, to walk around the square, buy something they wanted and, then come back to the van in about two hours. As a last-minute checkup, I asked the Kid what his name was and he smiled and said "W. R. Bird" and Apple Lisa picked it up and started chanting "Mr. Bird, Mr. Bird" and she dragged him off down the sidewalk to the store.

I stayed there, greeting the passersby, as I have done for years, making small talk, even stopping a farmer with what looked like twins, a boy and a girl about six years old and I asked him if they were twins and he said yes, and introduced the little girl as Judy and the little boy as Garland and I remarked on those names and told him I had once met twin boys named Mickey and Rooney and we said to each other, how remarkable it was, the effect that the movies had on us and by no more effort than that, I sold the old man three bundles of socks, three dollars' worth, fifteen pair or thereabouts. To tell you the truth, I have not really ever met twin boys named Mickey and Rooney and doubt if such a phenomenon exists anywhere in the world, but I excuse a little lightweight untruth on the grounds it leads to sales, and sales, as anyone will tell you, is what made this country great and keeps it rolling.

I ran into the usual eccentrics any roadside peddler meets in little towns on Saturday. For instance, two old sisters came along the sidewalk and stopped to see what I had for sale and I knew they were sisters because they looked so much alike and I could also tell they were very well off, if for no other reason than the rings they were wearing on their fingers, rubies, emeralds, and sapphires they were, or I have spent years dealing in precious stones and old gold along the road with no ability to recognize the real thing, to show for it.

These two old ladies took me for an educated man, which was certainly true by comparison with the average fifty-year-old man in that town, and talked about one thing and another and one of them said they moved back to Peasley Grove from Mobile, Alabama, because it was impossible to buy Bumble Bee tuna in Mobile, Alabama, the stores simply did not stock it and I chatted with them for a while and although they did not buy any socks, one of them dropped a twenty-dollar bill into the HELP US PAY FOR EYE SURGERY jug, which I planned to extract once back in Block Island and apply to the cost of another visit with Miss Eva Nell LaFangroy before I left that area for good.

At noon, I sent a man who had been hanging around, talking about his relatives, especially his brother Velvet, who had left home early, and who had gone up north "where he got eat by a pola bear" into the City Cafe with five dollars to get me a sandwich and a fried pie or two if he had enough money and I told him to get himself a pie and coffee, if he wanted. While he was gone, I sat down in a little folding chair I carry and wiped my forehead with a handkerchief, for it had begun to get hot, being an August afternoon in what I think was Arkansas, and it flashed across my mind that they had not come back yet, the Kid, that is, and Apple Lisa, and I stood up and looked each way up and down the street to see if I could see them. About that time, the man returned with my sandwich and two hot fried pies in a brown paper sack, with hot grease seeping through the bottom of it. I set the pies aside to cool and took a bite out of the sandwich which was some kind of spicy meat, a thick piece that was well cooked but had a texture unlike any meat I had ever eaten before. I asked the man what kind of a sandwich it was and he said, "Water buffalo," and I asked him, "Water buffalo?" and he said, "That's right. Since Gus Theopolis sold out to that Vietnam fella, that's all the meat they serve at the City Cafe." I set the sandwich aside, and took a bite of one of the fried pies, apple I think it was, but it tasted funny, too, another consequence of the Greek selling out to the Vietnamese, too much garlic, too many rose petals in it.

I was wondering what to do about something to eat for lunch, for I am a big man, used to eating my fill three times a day, and sometimes four or four and a half, and I did not plan to go hungry in Peasley Grove just because the City Cafe had changed hands, and I was thinking about shutting up the van, putting the socks back inside, and the table and the jug and the folding chair, and closing up for lunch, when that police car I had seen early in the morning drove up, skidded to a stop, and the policeman who had greeted me so eagerly earlier in the morning asked me, gruffly, if I had brought a young couple, a boy about twenty-three or so and a girl about eighteen into town with me, and I said, "Yes, they are some of our young people," but the policeman interrupted me and said never mind that, you need to get down to the jail, get in the car, I'll drive you. "Jail?" I asked, and the policeman nodded his head and said, "Them young people of yours are in jail!" and I do not need to tell you I knew it was over with, that I was caught, that

I faced years of hard labor, maybe the electric chair, if they could tie me in with the death of the Bunn brothers, and I just sort of sank into a stupor in the front seat of that squad car and did not say a word until I was taken into the courthouse, to the police department on the ground floor and taken up to a desk where a woman named Droola Patton, City Clerk, for such was the name on the plate at her desk, was looking busy and the policeman said to her, "Here is that Brother they said they were with." She looked up at me, did not smile or say a word, but got up and knocked on a door, then opened it and said to someone inside, "Senator, here's that Brother they said they were with."

Senator, I thought to myself, what sort of a mess are we all in? I happened to see the name State Senator J. W. "Birdbath" Scroggins on a desk pad and I assumed I was about to meet Senator Scroggins, whoever he was. Send him in, I heard the senator say and the woman stood back and let me into the office, where a man, about sixty-five, a good deal older than me, gray hair, wire-rim eyeglasses, and wearing one of those navy blue cloth caps with American Legion insignia on it, was sitting. I put out my hand to greet him and I said, "I'm Brother Edgar," and he stood up and shook hands and said "Brother, I don't want any trouble with the Catholic Church, but we've got a little problem here," and when he said that I knew it was not hopeless, it may not even be serious. I hardly heard him as he went on about some of the best people in Peasley Grove being Catholics and so on, but he said, those two kids with you, they have done something that has mightily offended the people here and I'd like to find out from you just what's wrong with them before I decide whether to turn them loose or not. I picked up right away that the Kid and Apple Lisa must have committed some misdemeanor, and I had an idea it was making love, or fucking, as they called it, in some public place, and that no one had discovered who the boy was, that he was the notorious White River Kid, wanted for killing six or eight. So all I said was, "Those two are some of our young people," and the senator picked up and said that's what we thought, some kind of retarded children or another, is that right, and I agreed it was right, that we Brothers have a ministry that works with retarded young people in the hopes of making them semi-self-supporting, and I could see the senator was buying it all, and I sensed that I was out of the woods on this. I asked him to tell me what they had done and he said he had been crossing the courthouse lawn about an hour earlier and had stopped, as he always does, to observe the cast aluminum free-form sculpture set up to honor the county's war dead, with its perpetual flame in eternal memory, and had been shocked to see two kids, a boy and a girl, frying bacon over the sacred flame.

At first, he was outraged at the mockery of the war monument, and ordered the two arrested and taken to jail where they were right now. After talking to them, he learned they were with the man selling socks, the Brother in the white van and they had sent for me. So that was all it was, I thought to myself, pure innocence, a problem brought on by unsophistication, by naïveté, and I started laying it on thick to the senator about the two young people, Mr. Bird and Miss Weed, about their being orphans, about their being, well, not all there, but we Brothers had great hopes of training them as hosiery technicians and how they did not have enough upstairs to be able to plot an act of mockery to the monument and they had no criminal intent, they simply did not know any better and I went on like that, and I could tell the senator was buying it, I was making it possible for him to excuse the behavior, and it looked like we were going to get away with no charges being pressed when the policeman told the senator it would take a couple hours work to get the bacon fat out of the gas jet that provided the sacred flame, not to mention the work of cleaning the grease off the monument itself. The senator was sort of stumped at that point and I volunteered the suggestion that the two be fined and the money could be spent to clean and relight the memorial flame and the senator bought it outright, even though he apologized for taking money from the Catholic Church, but I told him not to feel bad, that the Little Brothers of St. Mortimer paid their own way. Then I told him a movie

1 7 4

story, which is to say, I gave him a little fiction about how the Brothers in Chicago had had much the same problem when some of their young people, who were being trained as fishing tackle repairmen, tried out some fly rods in the municipal reservoir and caught fifty or so rare Japanese koi that the city had imported at great expense and how the Brothers had eagerly paid the city for the loss, realizing that there will be times when those whom the Brothers take under their wing will fall short.

So the upshot of my visit to Peasley Grove was that the White River Kid and Apple Lisa were fined fifty dollars each, money which I had to cough up from funds I had concealed in the van, but which I had there for just such unexpected expenses, and which I did not mind spending. The policeman took me downstairs to the jail and unlocked the cell where Apple Lisa was detained and she walked out, with no idea of what it had all been about, and then we went to the cell where the Kid was locked in with a punk kid who had been stopped when seen driving a new, expensive sedan automobile, which the policeman figured must be stolen because there was a strip on the bumper reading LET ME TELL YOU ABOUT MY GRANDCHILDREN. The Kid was almost paralyzed with terror and when he saw me he broke down and started sobbing and when he got out of that cell he hugged me and said he was sure glad to see me.

The three of us walked back to the van and got in and headed out of town, back to Block Island and Apple Lisa, as usual, got in one of the bunks and fell out, sound asleep, while the Kid sat in the seat opposite the driver. After we were well out of town, in fact, nearly home, nearly back to Block Island, he asked me why they had locked him in jail, and I tried to explain about his cooking bacon over the flame and how they thought he was making fun of the men who had been killed in the wars, and I went on awhile, but then realized he did not understand, he had no past experiences to tie any of it into and finally I said, I did not know why they had done it, but it was all over and they would never get him again and when he grasped that, he seemed to relax.

We got back to Block Island in time for supper, Sweet Sue

brand chicken and dumplings, which is probably the best canned food of any kind sold in this country today, and there was plenty for all because I had brought home four cans earlier in the week and asked Mrs. Weed to be sure she served it all, and she did along with more ice tea, and I put sugar in my glass until it was an inch thick at the bottom, then lemon, and then used the spoon to bring up some of the thick, syrupy sugar and eat it like candy.

The Kid hardly ate a thing, he was still so upset from having been locked away for that short time, two hours at the most, not long to an old lagg, an old lifer, like some of the fellows Doc Poole used to run around with, but too long for a free spirit like the White River Kid. Not only did he not eat, but he said almost nothing and what little he did say was said in a surly way, almost menacing, and I could see that the jail experience had set back all the good work I had tried to do as far as bringing him into society was concerned and I blamed myself for all the trouble, for I had given him ten dollars, which he and Apple Lisa had used to buy food in the first grocery story they came to, food, mind you, a strange thing to buy when both had had all the food they could eat at the Weed house and they were not in danger of being without any, but food, it was, bacon and cold drinks and candy bars and the Kid had tried to fry the bacon over the memorial flame by wrapping it around a green willow stick, maybe a way he had fried bacon, when he could get it, along the banks of the White River where he grew up. After supper, the Kid stayed in the house, sitting in the dark, and he sat there, by himself, even refusing Apple Lisa when she tried to pull him away, out of the house and into the woods behind it.

As usual, I went out on the front porch after supper and sat there and talked with Baker Weed and I told him the "young people" had got into a little trouble in Peasley Grove, nothing really bad, I said and then I gave him some of the details, skylarking around the war memorial, cooking bacon in the memorial flame, nothing more than that. I did not tell him Apple Lisa, his only daughter as far as I knew, had been locked up in a jail and he took it in stride. In fact, Baker Weed impressed me as a man who would always take everything in stride, nothing was going to get him off center and I guessed that might be the result of having had his father and grandfather vaporized one afternoon, when that aluminum plant down the road caught fire, while he was still young. I guess that after something like that happens to a boy, then nothing else that ever comes along will seem like all that much to him.

Mrs. Weed came out and sat with us on the porch, she had not cleaned up the supper dishes and the kitchen, as usual, and I saw that she was not wearing her Elvis Presley costume, she did not have on that jet black wig with the jet black sideburns, but instead, had on a flower print housedress and had her gray hair pulled together in a bun at the back of her head and that meant just one thing to me, that praying to Elvis Presley had not cured her cancer, that she was ready to give up on that notion. It was no surprise to me, a man who has seen many people in all stages of health in his life and if I had to make an educated diagnosis of her condition, I would say she was moribund, that she had about a year left to live, maybe not that long, and I based my guess on the fact that the tendons in the back of her neck were out, prominent as they could be, and I have always found that to be a sure sign of terminal illness. She sat there with us, a little old lady now that she was out of that ridiculous Elvis Presley Halloween costume, a frail woman, rocking and taking sips from a bottle of patent medicine called Syrup of Bohemia.

The Kid stayed in the house for the next two days, barely eating and not bathing, not talking to anyone, not even me, and I was getting worried about his mind. I thought he might be getting ready to go off and I thought it might be a good idea to take him on a little drive, a daylong trip, maybe, him and Apple Lisa, to, say, Hot Springs, where the Kid had had such a good time. I asked him if he would like to and he thought about it and his face sort of lit up and he said yes, he would like to see Hot Springs again and I said that would be my wedding present to him and Apple Lisa, that I would take them to Hot Springs in the morning, and see that they had a good time. Then I would pull out the next day, leave Block Island and get back to work and the Kid looked unhappy when I said I was leaving but I took his mind off of it by telling him I would be back through every two weeks or so and would always keep in touch with him and be there if he needed me.

Next morning, we all got up early, we all had cold baths in the bathroom with the spongy floor and the Kid and Apple Lisa dressed up in some of the clothes I had bought them and we drove to Hot Springs, Apple Lisa sleeping in the bunk and the Kid sitting beside me as I drove. He was not the old Kid I had come to feel good about, that experience in jail had really set him back and most of the time he just looked out the window, his face blank, his body tense, never smiling, most of the time not even responding to what I was saying to him.

We got to Hot Springs and first we drove up to the top of West Mountain and I took the Kid and Apple Lisa to the top of the Forest Rangers tower there in the elevator and they got a good view of the city and the horizon. Then we walked along Central Avenue, past the stores that had so delighted the Kid when we were there earlier but this time they were of no interest to him or to Apple Lisa, who was never interested in anything but sleeping and fucking. About noon, Apple Lisa (who I learned from Baker Weed had been named by Mrs. Weed after a French lady Mrs. Weed had met one afternoon when she was about eight months pregnant and who told Mrs. Weed her name, *"je m'appelle* Lisa," and Mrs. Weed had thought the name Apple Lisa was so pretty she decided to name her baby that if it was a girl, and it was) told me she wanted some catfish and she got insistent about it and so I looked around Hot Springs for a place that served catfish and finally found one, out near the race track and we three went inside and ordered catfish and hushpuppies and Apple Lisa ate hers but the Kid just pieced on his and I had to finish it up. After lunch, I drove them around some more, out to the lake, and around Burchwood Bay, then back to town and I was heading home when Apple Lisa said she wanted a Co-cola and I pulled into a little shopping center with a grocery store, an auto parts shop, a club or tavern of some sort, and a few other stores, a yarn shop, a Wal-Mart, the usual sort of shopping center one finds in a town the size of Hot Springs and I parked at the edge of the parking lot because there were lots of other cars there and I told Apple Lisa to go into the grocery store and get a cold drink and I gave her two dollars and then the Kid said he wanted a drink, too, so I gave him two dollars and they got out, while I waited at the wheel, and walked the fifty yards or so to the grocery store.

I was sitting up high in the Step Van, high enough to see them clearly as they walked together, the two of them, my family, as I had come to consider them and I followed them all the way with my eyes. I saw everything, I saw the door of the lounge next to the grocery store open, I saw a man come out of it carrying a small briefcase, I saw the Kid look at him, I saw the man look at the Kid, I saw the Kid pull that gun out of his belt and put it up to the man's head and I was horrified but I kept watching and I saw the man pull a gun out of his belt and point it at the Kid. They both fired about the same time and I saw the Kid's head look like it expanded, like someone had filled it up with air, then I saw it subside and I saw the Kid fall over and I knew he was dead and I knew the man was dead, too, for I had seen the back of his head blown out, blown away onto the sidewalk.

Apple Lisa was there, watching it all. When the Kid fell over she put her hand to her mouth and just stood there I would guess no more than five seconds, just looking at him and then to the other man and then, with some instinct born of being poor all the time, of never having anything, she reached down, picked up the briefcase the man had been carrying and slowly stepped around the side of the building and disappeared from my view.

I was shocked as I had never ever been shocked before. The Kid had the gun! I looked at the box under the bunk where I had put it away under lock and key and saw that the hasp had been pried off and was just hanging there.

Apple Lisa was gone and a crowd had started to gather,

people walking up to the scene of a tragedy slowly, gingerly, not wanting to see what was lying there on the sidewalk, but too curious to turn away, and too duty bound to ignore it, knowing somebody would have to report it to the authorities, make statements, be interviewed, maybe photographed for the newspapers and then have to clean up the mess.

I knew it was time for me to leave and I started the engine. No one noticed me on the edge of the parking area like I was, and I slowly eased out of the lot onto the highway and headed I knew not where. I was a block away from the shopping mall on the highway through town, when I saw her, Apple Lisa, standing on the side of the road, with the briefcase, hitchhiking. I stopped, opened the door, and she got in and sat down beside me, still holding the briefcase.

We drove a long time in silence then finally she spoke. "He's dead. That boy," she said. Many times in the past, I have had to console the bereaved and it has always been easy, I always had a few platitudes handy, a few social-worker type comments, such as "How do you feel about that?" This time I was not up to it for this time I too was bereaved, I had seen the nearest thing I will ever have to a son killed in front of my eyes and there was little I could say to Apple Lisa, but I tried, I finally did get hold of myself and I said, "I know. I know," and she nodded her head and sat there opposite me a while longer, then let go of the briefcase and went back to the bunk and fell asleep, while sucking her thumb.

The first thing I did was ease that briefcase out of sight under the seat and cover it up with some bundles of socks, then I kept on driving. We got back to Block Island around dark and I got out of the van and met Baker Weed and told him there had been a shooting scrape, and the Kid was dead and one other man, too, but that neither me nor Apple Lisa was involved in it and there would be no one coming to look for us, and he accepted it with his usual calm resignation, then went in the house and told Mrs. Weed and she came out to the van, woke up Apple Lisa, hugged her, and helped her into the house.

That night, as I lay in my bed in what now seemed to be an

1 8 0

uncomfortably hot room, with no breeze whatever coming in the window, I tried to piece things together, to determine what had happened. As I saw it, the Kid, terrified by his short time in jail in Peasley Grove, and regressing back to where he was the night I picked him up in the cafe, had become a wild thing again, and had gone out in the van, perhaps while we all slept, prized the lock off the box, taken out the gun I had hidden and brought it back to the house. When we left that morning for Hot Springs, it was tucked into his belt but I had not noticed it because he was wearing his shirttail outside his pants.

In Hot Springs, outside the grocery store, he had seen a man, the man who came out of the lounge carrying a briefcase, and had seen in his eyes the signs of another wooly gum and had instinctively pulled his gun to kill it, but the man was armed, too, for reasons I had not yet determined, and he seemed to actually be expecting some sort of attack such as the Kid presented and he pulled his gun and killed the Kid as the Kid killed him.

As far as I could tell, there was no danger of the authorities ever figuring out that the young man was the White River Kid, since he had no scar on his face, he had no identification on him, and had never been fingerprinted, and there were no known photographs of him in existence. Indeed, the Kid was wearing secondhand clothes, which might have had the previous owner's initials or name in them which would serve to throw off the authorities if they found them and tried to check them out. The only possible danger lay in the bullet from the Kid's gun, for if they ever compared it with the bullets that had killed those six or eight up along the White River, they would be onto the Kid for sure, although it would make no difference to him, since he was dead. Another real danger to my safety and freedom lay in the fact that the Kid had been arrested at Peasley Grove and while they did not fingerprint him there or as far as I know, even ask his name, someone from the police department there might remember his face and tie him in with "that fat Brother" but this was a risk I had to take. If I was ever questioned about it, I would say I had to get rid of the Kid and his girlfriend both, because they did not work out and I do not know what happened to them.

The next morning, I got up early, had breakfast, gave Baker Weed five pair of socks and a hundred dollars, which I told him was for my rent for the past two weeks, and I said good-bye to the Weeds and drove away, through Block Island and making a wide swing so I would not have to go through Socrates again, where that Marshal "I Love Puppies" might be on the lookout for me or my van in connection with the Bunn brothers and their having been eaten by wild hogs. I was fifty miles away from the house before I stopped along the road and took up the matter of the briefcase, which of course Apple Lisa had not remembered. It was locked but it was no obstacle to me, what with the tools I carry for repairing fishing tackle and in a minute I had it open.

Manila envelopes. At least thirty or thirty-five of them, with names on the outside of each, odd names sort of like codes, except one of them was familiar, it was "Birdbath" the same as the state senator in Peasley Grove who had ordered the arrest of Apple Lisa and the Kid. I knew at once there was money in those envelopes and when I opened the first one, I was proved right. There was money in each one, different amounts in each. Obviously I had fallen into possession of a lot of money that someone outside the law was planning to pay to the bosses, the police, the powers that be. I closed up the briefcase and put it back under the pile of socks and drove on, looking for a safe motel, where I could examine it in detail.

The reason the man killed by the Kid had a gun was because he was some sort of runner for the Mob, if you can glorify the criminal element in Hot Springs with such a title and the reason he shot, even though the Kid had a gun on him, was he was a professional mobster. That must be the explanation, he was hired for his courage, he was used to having guns shoved in his face and shooting his way out.

I found a motel about ten miles along the way, new, clean, safe looking, and I registered as Brother Edgar, and took my luggage, including the briefcase, inside. I locked the door, sat down at the table, and emptied out the envelopes filled with money, opened them all, put the envelopes in a neat stack, so there would not accidentally be one left behind, and then started to count the money.

One hundred seventy-one thousand dollars! I had trouble breathing and I felt my temples get tight and was afraid I was going to stroke out but I went into the bathroom, wet my face in cold water, and lay on the bed a minute, pondering my good fortune. I stayed there all day and all that night, at first, scared of every noise I heard, afraid the mob had found out I had the money and was coming to get it, but after a while, I relaxed and told myself, I was in no danger, no one knew I had the money, no one ever would.

Next morning, I got up, took a shower, then cut the briefcase into small ribbons of leather and put them and the envelopes in a brown paper bag and tucked it under my seat in the van, then I locked away the money in one of the safety boxes I had welded to the body of the van. I left and drove to a little grocery store where I bought a package of frankfurters, a package of hot dog buns, and a can of charcoal lighter. A few miles down the road, I came to one of those little roadside rest stops where they have grills for cooking out. I put the package of shredded briefcase and the envelopes into one of the grills, doused it with charcoal lighter, and set fire to it. It all burned up in a few minutes, completely turned to ash, no trace of the case or the envelopes left, then I put some firewood on the grill, lit it with the charcoal lighter and roasted a couple hot dogs, just for appearance' sake.

All this took place three years ago. The authorities in northwest Arkansas are still looking for the White River Kid, and I presume the Mob is still looking for its money but are baffled by the fact that some farmer, some rat-faced boy whom no one recognized, who could not possibly have known when the delivery was to be made, was there to get it, because of what it was, cash money bribes to the leading politicians in the area, and who must have had an accomplice because the briefcase was missing. Of course, no one but me knew that the White River

Kid had no idea there was money in that bag, all he knew was there was another wooly gum who had to be freed.

And so, I think I have got away with it, over one hundred seventy thousand dollars all in cash, all I am sure in unmarked bills, all genuine United States currency with a little age on it and while I am sure there are some who would say I have had such good luck because I took a poor country boy under my wing and tried to help him and that the Fates are being good to me, but that is nonsense.

I have observed that a man can go all his life never doing anything but good to others and ninety-nine times out of a hundred he will die broke, unloved, unappreciated, maybe even spat upon by those he helped. Everything in this life is pure chance, there is no order, and there is no reward for the good and no punishment for the evil.

As far as the world knows, the White River Kid is alive, up there along the White River, still lurking in the shadows with the means and desire to kill another six or eight and it is my intention to let that stand. I am the only one on the face of the earth who knows the White River Kid is dead and I intend to keep it a secret because that will ensure he lives, at least, in the imagination of people.

Every time there are ripples in the water, every time fish are stolen off a trot line, every time there are strange footprints in the mud, every time a dog howls on a dark night, every time a man is shot to death with no witnesses, they will say it is the White River Kid, on the prowl again, and that way he will become part of folklore, alongside Billy the Kid and Jesse James, and someday they will make a movie about him.

I know I have disgraced the Little Brothers of St. Mortimer by my lawbreaking, my fornication, and by my keeping the money. I am sure Mortimer Snerd would condemn me and Edgar Bergen would be repelled by what I have done but I think Charlie McCarthy would be proud of me.